DEDICATION

For Ted, thank you for putting up
with my constant complaints on
how much I hate writing.

And thanks to the fine people
of NZI Support who unknowingly
lent their names to the first draft.

Hopefully, I've edited you all out.

Found, Near Water

KATHERINE HAYTON

ISBN: 0473279932
ISBN-13: 978-0-473-27993-6

CONTENTS

CHAPTER ONE

I set out the chairs in a circle. In my head I counted off each person as I placed their seat. Terry, dead daughter; Ilene, missing daughter; Kendra, missing daughter; Joanne, sick daughter; Christine, dead daughter. That last one is me, by the way.

There used to be a need for more chairs. I had quite the group running at one stage. Not now. We've dwindled and whittled our way to a close knit bunch. Like a knitting circle with barbed tongues driving all the young and optimistic members away.

I remember when I was talked into setting up this group. I was whining away to an old colleague one day and she mentioned that I may be helped by a support group. A fucking support group! I "reminded" her that I was a fully qualified psychiatrist who had once had a roaring career until I realised how futile the entire field was. I wasn't someone who attended a support group. I was the one to run it.

Famous last words.

There was a crunch of gravel outside and I walked to the window to have a nosey. Not one of mine. An elderly gent made slow progress towards the temporary library. He swayed so deeply from foot to foot he looked like a Weeble in full wobble.

I hadn't gotten home until late last night. Usually I'd pull together something for us few to snack on, but I couldn't be bothered by the time I got in. Gary woke me on his way out, but I was too tired and too grumpy to be bothered this morning either.

I laid out a half packet of stale gingernuts which had mysteriously survived in our pantry and hoped that no one was feeling too hungry.

There was still another five minutes before anyone was due, and it would probably be longer before they all showed up. I sat down heavily in a chair and dragged my fingers through my hair. I felt rough, ragged. All I really wanted to do was go back home and cook something solid for tea. Something with vegetables instead of vegetable oil. Sit down with Gary and catch up with him. It seemed like it had been weeks since we'd done more than nod at each other in the hallway. Seemed like? No, it had been.

I pulled out my phone and sent him a quick text. *Fancy a nite out?* My battery was getting low. I'd forgotten to charge it up yesterday.

'Cheerio love. Got the coffee on yet?'

Kendra went straight to the machine and started it up. I don't know why she bothered to ask – I preferred instant and had never got the hang of machines no matter how simple others kept explaining they were.

'How's your week been?' she asked as she leant back against the counter.

'Nothing much. I seem to recall getting a good night's sleep over a week ago, and that's about it.'

'Any new clients?'

I shrugged. There'd been some, but no one needing more than a few hours support so below the unspoken criteria.

There was a snort from the doorway as Terry made her way into the room. 'Clients, huh? Thought they were victims?'

'Not very PC love.'

'Whatever. You'll never guess what I found out today.'

I looked at her closely. The tone of her voice was off from the usual. Cynicism was her chief reaction to life, but now she had a measure of excitement. Excitement tinged with something else that I couldn't put my finger on. Terry's usually dull complexion was flushed with red as though she'd been sitting in front of a heater for too long.

'What's that?'

'They've released him.'

Kendra dropped a teaspoon into the sink, swore, and flinched against the noise. 'Released who?' she asked idly as she fished down into the disposal unit to try to retrieve her cutlery.

I stared at her as reality dawned.

Kendra was still fiddling about at the sink. 'Released who?' she repeated, and then turned around as the silence lengthened.

'Oh shit.'

Terry nodded.

'But it's only been six years, hasn't it?'

Terry nodded. Her colour may have been high already, but she still managed to grow more flushed by the second.

'Six years, five months and twenty three days,' she whispered.

'Shit,' Kendra repeated, and then moved across the room to pull Terry to her in a hug. A hug that was not in any way reciprocated.

'God's sake Kendra, let her go. You'll strain yourself.'

Kendra released Terry, but kept a hand on her arm until Terry shook it off with irritation. She'd never been one for physical contact. At least, not with her own gender.

'How did you find out?' I asked.

'Hey, have you started without me again,' Ilene said as she walked in. Her smile dropped away as she looked at each of us in turn. 'What's happened?'

Terry opened her mouth to speak, but Joanne appeared at the doorway as well, and her jaw slammed shut again.

'Am I late?' she asked as she tip-toed across the room. Joanne held her arms folded over in front of her stomach. Her shoulders hunched in.

3

'No, you're right on time. How are you feeling?'

Joanne sat on the edge of a chair, and then placed her hands underneath her thighs. She breathed out and there was a tremor that shook her tiny frame.

'Not good.'

Joanne tried to move her mouth to say more but all that emerged was a whimper. She angrily wiped tears away from her eyes, but she was fighting a losing battle.

'The treatment's not taking,' she managed finally. 'She isn't coming back like she has the other times. She's just getting sicker and sicker.'

She paused and there was another struggle for control.

'Take your time,' I said into the silence. It sounds awful but I was bored with this. I'd watched so many parents struggle to deal with their sick children, their dying children. My empathy was used up.

I wanted to hear what Terry had to say.

'The doctors want to pull her treatment altogether. They said that it's no longer going to work and it would just make her sicker during the time that she has left.'

I nodded. It sounded about right.

Ilene stepped in with some sympathy thank God. 'That must be such a hard decision to make,' she offered. 'I don't think any one of us would be able to make it lightly.'

Joanne nodded and pulled her hands from under her thighs to cross them over her stomach again. 'I keep thinking that they must be wrong. If I just give her another day, another week, it'll begin to work. She'll have more time.'

Ilene put her hand out on Joanne's arm. 'Do you think that's possible?'

Joanne sniffed loudly and tilted her head back so that gravity helped to stop everything flowing.

'I don't know. I don't know. What do you think?'

Her head was still tilted back. The question went out to everyone in the room, but fell to the floor unclaimed.

Ilene sat back in her chair, her hand no longer offered. 'It's not our place to say.'

'Well what would you do?'

'I wouldn't have her in the hospital in the first place. Those bloody doctors. You can't trust them for a second.'

Kendra closed her eyes and shook her head theatrically. Joanne just looked nonplussed. She hadn't been around for long enough to strike Ilene's adverse opinion of the medical sciences before.

The rest of us; water off a duck's back. Even me, and I used to be a member of the hated group.

'Christine? What do you think?'

Poor Joanne. Her daughter is spending her days with last-chance poison dripping into her veins, and we barely acknowledge her and her pain. Too used to being caught up in our own.

I looked at her straight in the eyes. There would be few enough people making eye contact with her in the weeks and months to come. No one likes to look into the face of grief.

'I think that your daughter's doctors are acting in her best interests. You don't need to follow their advice, but I don't think they're wrong. There's a small chance you might extend your daughter's life with treatment, but there's a big chance you'll just hurt her and it won't make any difference.'

Joanne looked back at me for long seconds. She then turned and looked at each member of the group in turn.

'None of you really care, do you?'

Kendra opened her mouth to say yes, but her head was already shaking no.

Terry looked like she hadn't even heard, and Ilene just looked like she was considering extolling some more on the evils of modern medicine.

'We feel for you, we really do,' I supplied. I forgot to inject any emotion in my voice, but I went through the motions.

Joanne looked down at the ground for a moment, then stood and walked out without saying another word.

Ilene shrugged as the door closed behind her. 'She didn't last long.'

'Yeah, well you might have tried a bit harder,' Kendra bit back at her.

'Me? You practically pushed her out.'

'Oh shut up both of you. I don't know why you keep trying to introduce new people into our group anyway,' Terry said, her accusing gaze falling on me. 'They're always so self-obsessed. It's not as though they're adding anything.'

Kendra gave a short laugh. 'And now you have the stage, my dear...?'

'Well about time. They've released Martin.'

'How did you find that out?' I asked, and received a narrowed look in response.

'I found it out when the probation service contacted me as a courtesy to let me know of their decision. As I'd attended his hearing and made it quite clear that he should never be released into the general population ever in his life they thought I'd like to know they'd completely ignored everything I had to say and were letting him loose.'

'Shit,' Ilene contributed. 'I thought they had ways of keeping them locked up longer these days.'

'They do,' I said. 'But I imagine the fact he was a teenager at the time swayed them.'

'Yeah, because it's fine to murder and rape when you're nineteen, but at twenty you should be locked away forever.'

'Where's he going?'

Terry shook her head. 'They won't tell me that. Apparently he has to stay well away from me, not that there's anything left for him to harm anyhow.'

'Probably to protect him more than anything,' Kendra threw in.

'Yeah, well he fucking better stay away from me. Otherwise he'll be sorry.'

'Have they already released him?' I asked. 'Or were they just letting you know it's about to happen.'

'They let him go Wednesday. Last Wednesday. Just set him free.'

There was silence for a few minutes. The mid-morning sun had started to come through the grimy windows. It felt hot on my back and reminded me that summer was on its way.

'You could ask someone where he was staying,

couldn't you?' Terry asked me. 'You work with the police after all.'

'I work in the same office. I don't work with them. And they won't know anything more than the probation officers have told you. Separate services. You'd need to get to know someone in corrections.'

'Sleep with a jailer, you mean.'

'Give your CO a seeing to,' Ilene chimed in and I started to laugh.

'Screw a screw,' Kendra said, and then wrinkled up her nose.

I laughed harder and then couldn't stop. It must've been infectious because soon the whole circle was in hysterics. Even Terry.

There was a slam as the door opened again and Joanne walked back into the room. She glared at us all, and stomped over to her chair. She pulled a light scarf from the back which I hadn't even noticed she'd left behind, and then walked quickly back out. I couldn't help myself. It was so ridiculous I started to laugh again, my stomach aching, my chest heaving for air, tears running down my cheeks.

***

When I walked into the police station at 12.30 pm there was a buzz in the air. I ignored it, and took my seat at my desk. If I pretended to care, the bastards I worked beside day in and day out would make a point of torturing me by never letting me know what was going on. If I kept schtum and showed no interest I could eavesdrop and find out what was what in the matter of a few minutes.

Except this time I didn't have to wait.

'Christine,' Erik Smith called out just as I sat down. 'Come over here.'

I didn't work for the police. I was a victim support counsellor and co-ordinator for the North Christchurch region. Apart from sharing their office space and occasionally a recommendation for help I had nothing to do with the police really.

It didn't matter. Detective Senior Sergeant Erik Smith acted like a bit of a prick; but at heart that was because he was a bit of a prick. If someone was within summoning distance of him then he felt comfortable doing so. Even if that someone had explained over and over the process and procedures for recommendations. How they weren't his lackey. How he didn't have hierarchy over them because they weren't part of his club.

Deaf ears. Extremely large and unflattering deaf ears.

I sat mulishly behind my desk for a minute more, and then responded to him. It was just easier. And I was curious.

'What?' I may have followed his orders, but I didn't need to be pleasant.

'Got a case for you. Needs a bit of a delicate touch. Feely-feely all that.'

I held out my hand for the details. He should've had them written out on the referral card, but of course that was hoping for too much.

He snorted in mockery.

'It's the one on the news at the moment. Mrs Sutherland.'

I shrugged my shoulders and raised my eyebrows. I had no idea.

'Thought the extent of your social life was watching the telly Christine?'

I shrugged again. The teeth biting back my sarcasm drew blood from the side of my cheek. Bright, metallic blood. I wished it belonged to someone else.

'What about the papers? You read the papers?'

'God's sake Erik. Just tell me what it is.'

He creased his forehead and looked over my shoulder with his mouth pursed. 'Detective. Senior. Sergeant,' he said with slow emphasis. 'Now you try it.'

'For god's sake Detective Senior Sergeant, just tell me what you want.'

He smiled and made eye contact with me again. Joy.

'There's this crazy woman. In the hospital. Got hit by a car. She reckons her kid's missing.'

I nodded, and then frowned. I had read about this

one actually. 'She's the one who's been missing for a lot longer? Is that right?'

Erik nodded and passed over a name and ward number from the hospital.

'Thing is, we don't actually know if she's telling us the truth or not.'

I looked at the information for a moment, then frowned up at him as his words registered. 'And..?'

'Well. You know how you used to be a shrink?'

'Detective Senior Sergeant, I am not an employee of the police. If you want to work out if she's telling the truth or not then pay someone on your staff to do it.'

'We've tried. There's no one available until tomorrow who's even remotely qualified.'

'So wait until tomorrow.'

'If this child is actually missing then we need to allocate a lot more resource than we've got available. If I am to request that I need to be certain that there's actually a missing child somewhere in the mix otherwise I'm going to get my bollocks chewed off.'

I couldn't really see the downside.

'What is the alternative? You think she's made a child up out of thin air?'

He shook his head. 'No, but her ex-husbands over in Australia. Travels there quite a lot. Her mother's off on a cruise. Apparently she spends a lot of time overseas as well. We can't find anyone who's close to her or her ex-husband to confirm what the status is with regard to custody, and there's been a case in the courts saying that she's a nutter and she shouldn't have any custody.'

'Well, if it's been through the courts...'

'Her husband didn't mention any daughter when the hospital rang him as next of kin to say his wife's been brought in unconscious. Officers have gone through her home and say it looks like no one lives there, let alone a small child. If she is genuinely missing then we need to get onto it full-force straight away because the odds are already stacked against us, but for the time being we don't know if we're chasing a ghost or what.'

'If I go in there I'm there as her support. It's confidential. I can't pass information onto you just because it makes your job easier.'

'I'm not asking for a full run-down on the conversation. I just want some sort of indication that she's telling the truth and at the moment I can't get it. There's something off and until I feel more confident I'm not happy about pulling officers out of genuine crime cases in order to pursue this.'

I stared at the details for another long moment.

'Please Christine. You're going there anyway. All I want is your professional opinion as to whether she's genuine. After all, if she's not you're not going back either are you?'

'Fine, but I don't expect to hear about this in the future okay?'

'Wouldn't dream of it.'

'Can I get a lift to the hospital then? My car's on its last legs.'

He laughed, and walked away shaking his head.

So glad I could do him a favour.

***

Ugh. Hospitals. The smell of illness and antiseptic. The pale green walls. The weird conglomeration of signs that lead you around the maze of corridors and lifts and then abandon you just as you seem to be getting close. All the sick people who look up with hope and expectation in their faces as you pass by. Ugh. Sick people.

I checked in with reception, and was directed to ICU. After wandering for a while, then following a red line on the lino, I found the correct section.

'Excuse me,' a nurse called as I came through into the adjoining room. 'Are you here for Rena Sutherland?'

I nodded.

'Would you mind waiting in the friends and whanau room for a moment. There's just a few things we need to prepare before she can see you.'

Prepare what? It didn't bear thinking about it, so I didn't. Instead I turned back and entered the room to the left. There were soft cushions on sofas, and a variety of magazines the hospital seemed to have gotten second hand from a dentist's waiting room. I sat and picked up a reader's digest. August 2006. How relevant.

I pulled my phone out of my pocket and registered the blinking blue light with dismay. I hadn't even heard it ring. There was a poster on the wall with a cross through a picture of a cell phone, but I ignored it for the time being. It seemed years since anyone had taken much trouble to enforce the ban.

Not tonight. Working late.

Great. Another day where I wouldn't get to see the man I'd sworn in front of family and God that I would love forever. It was starting to seem more like we were flatmates than married.

I thought about texting him back, but I was too tired to think of anything witty, and I felt too disgruntled to say anything caring. What on earth did he mean he was working late anyway? Gary didn't spend much time working even when he was meant to. Thanks to the Christchurch housing market, commissions just fell into his lap. Was he being sarcastic? Stuff him then. I'd have a nice meal by myself. And maybe a bottle of wine.

I stood up and paced the small room. My usual place of work was in people's homes, in their lounges, in their conservatories, meeting them at their local whether that was a coffee shop or a bar. It had been a long time since I'd been in a hospital, and my memories of the places weren't great.

Hopefully she'd be mad and this would be a one-stop shop. Or she'd be perfectly sane, and well on the mend, and the next visit would be at her nice little three bedroom summerhill stone house. Or whatever she passed off as her home.

A doctor knocked on the door and I opened it cautiously.

'Hi,' she said walking forward so that I fell back automatically. 'I just wanted to have a quick chat before you see Ms Sutherland.'

'I'm not family,' I interjected. There were privacy laws that I didn't want accidentally bowled over in a case of mistaken identity.

The doctor nodded her head. 'Nevertheless if you want to see Ms Sutherland you'll need to be aware of a few things. She'll tire easily – she's just been through an enormous trauma and her body still has a long way to go before recovering – so if she asks you to leave I need you to respect that.'

I nodded. 'I'm here from victim support so I'm not going to stay unless Rena wants me to stay. I won't do anything that violates that arrangement.'

I should've had my fingers crossed behind my back on that one, although Erik was right. If Rena was "mistaken" about the whole thing then I wasn't going to be supporting her through her imaginary ordeal, just as the police wouldn't be following up on an imaginary missing person.

'She also has a support nurse beside her at all times. That's for her own safety to monitor her condition. If her nurse feels that you're aggravating her situation then she'll ask you to leave. I need you to follow that request also.'

'I used to be a doctor myself,' I replied. 'I'm not going to do anything that puts her health in jeopardy.'

'I said that I need you to follow that request also.'

Fine. If she was just going to ignore the sisterhood then I wouldn't bother either.

'Of course. I'll follow any of your directions unless Rena asks me otherwise.'

'Ms Emmett. Ms Sutherland is a seriously ill woman and I'm sure we all only want what is best for her wellbeing. Even if she thinks it's in her best interests for you to stay I need to have your agreement that you'll follow the hospital staff instructions.'

Well that was me told. I nodded wearily. This all seemed like too much trouble all of a sudden. I thought of Joanne and how I'd treated her this morning. There wasn't much use in me continuing to offer support if I couldn't provide it. Maybe it was time for me to seek another line of work.

'Come on through then.'

I walked through into the room before ICU again. There were large signs on the walls and the doors announcing that I should wash my hands before entering. As I coated my hands with soap I felt a pang of homesickness to the days of my residency. Back then the world had seemed so full of wonder and promise. Wide open with all of the choices that I could make. Every year since it had shrunk a little smaller. I scrubbed up in the sink and pulled a couple of paper towels to wipe my hands dry again. The connecting door was on a sensor so that I didn't have to place my newly angelic flesh on anything before I was in the ICU proper.

There were six beds in the room, every single one of them full. With the attending nurse positioned at each bedside, and a small room with another head nurse stationed, it felt claustrophobically overcrowded. Machines were hooked up to every bedside with muted sounds marking progress or regress at low volume in deference to the unconscious or sleeping patients.

Rena made eye contact with me as soon as I walked through the door. As well as looking to be the only awake patient in the room, she was also half-propped up in bed but not due to her own mobility. Someone had raised the head of the bed so she was almost in a sitting position.

Bruises leaked colour out from their originating point to the corners of her face. Some overlapped on her cheeks. Bright purple. Grey-green. A line of blood red.

The side of her head was shaved, and a line of stitches marked the territory of a head injury. Beautiful long blond hair was pulled back from the opposite side. Rena may not even be aware of it at the moment, but I bet that would be heart-breaking to get used to. A sling held her left arm close to her chest, and the sheet lay in perfect outline for a metal cage that marked the full length of her left leg.

My information showed Rena's age to be forty-one, but lying back against the pillows, even with worry lines biting into the soft curves of her skin, she didn't look out of her twenties.

There didn't look to be an inch of her that wouldn't be screaming with pain, but the on-call morphine pump to her side showed that she had pain relief to spare. That, and the quick way her eyes tracked my movement, were good signs for her cognitive abilities. The choice to endure pain over comfort for the sake of remaining sharp was a hard call. And not one that anyone would make voluntarily without reason.

'Hi Rena? I'm Christine. I'm from Victim Support and I'm here to help you in any way you feel comfortable.'

I looked to shake her hand or touch her arm, make some sort of initial contact, but every part of her that my eyes fell on seemed to have some form of injury. I waved a greeting instead.

'Are you happy for me to take a seat here with you?'

Rena started to nod, but then winced and held her head still. Vice-like still. 'Yes,' she replied instead.

There was a plastic chair that I dragged into position beside her bed. It was odd to sit to one side, my attention on her, while on her other side her dedicated nurse did the same. Not the place I could expect to get a full list of confessions, but privacy was only for the able bodied after all. It doesn't take long in a hospital to work that one out.

'How are you coping?'

'Have you talked to the police? Do you know what they're doing?'

I shook my head, and then realised that Rena wouldn't be able to see me from her angle. 'No, I haven't really spoken with them. They're investigating. That's all I know.'

'She's been gone for so long. I can't believe that Ash didn't tell anyone.'

'Is that your husband?'

'Ex-husband. Yes.'

Rena's fingers tapped out a quick pattern on the bedspread. A complicated manoeuvre that involved all four fingers and thumb in rotation, and then in some more complex routine. I couldn't follow the motions, but I knew that they were forming a repeated pattern the same way you can watch a performer on screen and know if they're playing the piano or just pretending to while music is overlaid on the soundtrack.

'How do you feel about your daughter's disappearance?'

Rena snorted and winced again with the movement it involved.

'I don't feel very good Christine. I'm trapped in a bed and I can barely move and my daughter is missing and has been for days and I don't feel good at all.'

'Is it possible that Ash didn't realise she was missing?'

Rena pushed her head further back into the pillows. 'I don't know where else he thought Chloe would be. I don't really know anything. I'm just taking the hospital's word for it that they even called him.'

Rena's nurse frowned at the affront to her organisation's truthfulness, but she visibly bit back a retort.

'I'm sure that they're telling the truth to the police. They'll be able to check.'

Rena's fingers tapped out the pattern once more. There was a pause for a few minutes, and then the pattern came again.

I looked at her closely, and then took a punt on my own assessment.

'Rena, I don't want you to take this the wrong way, and I'm not ascribing any judgement, but have you ever been diagnosed with a mental illness?'

Her fingers tapped out the pattern again, twice in quick succession, and then twice again after a short pause.

'It depends what you mean by a mental illness.'

'I mean something that may result in you keeping your house unusually clean. Something that might mean you have compulsions that you need to carry out otherwise you feel you're placing people around you in danger.'

I thought of what Erik had said about the officers going through her home. Looking at a room built for a child, but which it didn't appear any child lived in. Too clean. Too neat. Too tidy.

'I've been treated for depression before. Is that what you're after?'

'I'm not really after anything Rena. I'm sorry if I've made you feel uncomfortable. Please don't answer me if you don't feel it's appropriate.'

The tension that had been building in the lay of Rena's body started to leave again.

'I don't really know what help you people offer,' she said. 'I've never been in any sort of situation like this before.'

'I can help you with anything that springs to mind. If you want me to sit with you and let you talk, then I'll do that. If you want me to help you take care of some practical matters I can do that too.'

'And if I've been mentally ill then what?'

I sat back in the chair. 'If you've been mentally ill then I'll watch out for you, and I'll sit here and listen if you need to talk, and if you want me to help you take care of some practical matters I can help with that.'

There was silence for a long time. At least there was silence from Rena. The rest of the room quietly hummed with low activity as before.

'I don't really remember what happened before today. I remember that I was next to the car. I think I remember some sounds. But I can really only think of waking up here early this morning.'

'That must be very frightening for you.'

'It is. And then I couldn't speak for ages. There was a tube down my throat. I thought I was choking.'

'Was that for your breathing?'

'Yes. For my breathing,' she paused. 'The first thing I asked when they took the tube out was where Chloe was. They didn't know anything about her. That scared me more than anything ever has before.'

I stretched out and took the pattern tapping hand in mine, and stroked it gently. It was as bruised and misshapen as the rest of Rena, but if she could stand the pain of it tapping out a calming rhythm on the spread, then I figured it could stand up to being held. Her fingers jerked in surprise, and then relaxed.

'I've been diagnosed with OCD. It gets pretty bad at times. It's the main reason why Ash fought me for custody. At least I think it is. He doesn't discuss anything with me anymore. He stopped well before he decided he wanted a divorce.'

I thought back to my text from Gary. I knew how that

went.

'I know I've been hit on the head. It hurts like hell. I know that I've got a mental illness and that both of these things make what I say suspect in the eyes of people around me. But I'm not lying about my daughter Christine,' she stated as she met my eyes. Her hand squeezed mine. 'Chloe was with me that day. She was in the back seat of the car. And if she wasn't involved in the accident, and she wasn't picked up by the ambulance or police staff, then she's been missing for four days.'

She swallowed and I could see her throat working against itself. She pulled her hand free from mine and started to tap again.

'Four days. I'm not stupid Christine. I know that if my daughter has been missing for that long then she's in deep trouble. Deep, deep, trouble.'

A monitor to Rena's side started to beep a warning sound. I turned to it as the nurse leaned forward and reset it. The sound came again after a minute.

I knew what was coming before the hand landed on my shoulder.

'I think it's time for you to leave.'

***

"Please leave a message..."

'Erik, it's Christine here. I've spoken with Rena. She's clear, competent and her recall is on track.' I paused for a moment as I tried to think how to convey the message in the right way. 'You need to start throwing resources into this. That girl's really missing.'

CHAPTER TWO

Terry's Story

I had Jacob early, before I was ready maybe. I don't mean I didn't want him, and once I found out I was pregnant I didn't even think of terminating the pregnancy. Not even once. But I was young, and I was stupid, and I did not know how to be a mother. Not at all.

When he was little I was stressed all the time. I was stressed about whether I was doing everything wrong or not. I was stressed about having to think of my son all of the time whether I wanted to or not. I was stressed about how I was ever going to afford everything everyone seemed to think I needed to raise Jacob without him turning into a serial killer rapist monkey boy.

I took so much time and energy worrying about what I was doing wrong that I never really took the time to enjoy him. I didn't enjoy him growing bigger and stronger. I didn't enjoy any of his milestones. He was just there all the time, the source of all my worry and regret and the life I thought I was going to lead until he arrived. I don't think I wrecked him, but I'm pretty sure I didn't structure his life in the way a good parent is meant to.

Emma was my second chance. I planned her birth and worried when I didn't conceive right away. I had money put aside so that I never had to worry about whether or not I should buy one thing over another; I could just buy both. I put her room together the way I had imagined my perfect room would be when I was a girl myself.

When she was born she was a good baby. Not fussy the way Jacob had been. She woke in the night, of course she did, but only once or twice and once I gave her a feed and a cuddle she would fall straight back to sleep.

Even Jacob loved her. I'd been worried that with the age difference he might resent her. I'd been worried that after fourteen years of being an only child he would be out of sorts with the new arrival. But that didn't happen. Jacob fell in love with his little sister as quickly as I did, and he was a wonder when it came to helping her out. He still wouldn't lift a finger to help me, he was a teenager after all, but he would do anything I asked him if it helped out Emma.

He changed her, he comforted her, he fed her bottles that had been cautiously warmed to just the right temperature.

That was why I felt okay about going back to work part time. I would handover when Jacob got home from school, and he would take care of Emma for three nights each week while I acclimated back into the adult world.

Our little family functioned on in this manner for the next couple of years. Jacob grew facial hair and at least a foot taller. He started to attend university with immense enthusiasm, and Emma started school with immense trepidation, but otherwise we just potted along.

And then on the fifteenth of March 2007 I came home after a short day's work, and Emma wasn't there. Jacob was, but he was unconscious on the bed and from the smell of him he hadn't got to that state accidentally.

There were the police asking endless questions. There was the media attention and my daughter's photo pasted across the front page of a lot of newspapers. She didn't look anything like those photos. She was living, breathing, full of motion and life and energy. She would snuggle in next to me on a weekend morning and run a length of my hair through her pudgy wee hands and exclaim in admiration 'Mummy. You're so pretty.'

I thought that not knowing was the worst thing I could ever endure. Not knowing if she was in trouble or needing my help or in pain. I worried that she'd been taken by someone that would hurt her, then I worried that she'd been taken by someone who would love her and care for her and in a year or two she'd have forgotten I ever existed. Not knowing was killing me.

But it turned out that knowing was far worse. When I went to the hospital to identify my beautiful girl's broken body - that was worse than not knowing. When I buried her in the cemetery and compared the size of the gravesite to the other freshly buried bodies - that was worse than not knowing. When I drank myself to sleep on a anniversary of her sixth birthday, and realised that I would likely be doing that until my life ended - that was worse than not knowing.

The police had found her body stuffed into an old recycling bin out the back of a sleep-out. My beautiful girl had been bent to fit as though she was just a piece of rubbish, something to be disposed of. The sleep-out belonged to a friend of Jacob. They'd been in the same class at school together since intermediate. They hung out often. Maybe not every week, but certainly every month. I'd said hello to him more times than I could remember. I'd come out to ask if they wanted a snack, or to ask if it was alright with his mother if he stayed for tea, or to check that they were okay in their sleeping bags when he stayed over and they wanted to pretend they were camping.

I'd done all those things, and he'd fed my son a small shot of bourbon that he'd stolen out of his dad's stash of alcohol. A small shot laced with four Zopiclone tablets that had knocked my poor boy out like a light. The same tablets had been used to subdue my precious baby girl. He'd stolen them from his parent's medicine cabinet because they were too stupid or preoccupied or just fucking uncaring to even notice if someone was taking drugs out of their cabinet. And why did they even have a prescription for them if they weren't taking them? What kind of stupid were they?

He used them to subdue her while he carried out the sick fantasies that filled his head where good common decency should've been. And he'd used too many on one occasion and she died and he still kept her in the sleep-out that he lived in like some kind of hobo while her body stiffened with rigor mortis, and then softened again. While her stomach started to protrude with gasses as the bacteria inside her started to feed unchallenged by any of her living functions. While her eyeballs deflated and her tongue turned black and her sweet girl smell turned into a stench of decay. And when he didn't have any further use for her he put her body into a plastic green recycling bin and knowing all of that was worse than not-knowing.

Martin Hinks. That was the name of the shitty sub-human pervert that stole Emma away from me. Stole Jacob too because it grew too hard to look at him after a few weeks. After all he'd brought that man into our lives and he'd let him take away my baby girl when he was meant to be looking after her. And yes – I know that's not fair, but knowing something's unfair doesn't stop it from happening. My psychologist keeps repeating how important it is to make Jacob know that it wasn't his fault; that deviants can hide in any community group undetected because they're not monsters it's just the things that they do are monstrous. I should direct my anger and sorrow at the target who's actually responsible for the pain that I feel. But there's so much to go around. So much.

And no one thinks Mummy's beautiful anymore.

CHAPTER THREE

'Hey Christine. Got your message. Think she's ready for a live broadcast?' Erik cornered me before I could get back to my desk. 'The media are breathing down my neck and better to use them than have them piss me off for nothing.'

I was tired already, and annoyed that the nurse had chucked me out of Rena's room before I was ready to leave. And before she'd had a chance to use me for any support as well.

'I'm not in a position to be able to tell you that. I thought you were going to arrange someone to advise you in relation to Rena. Shouldn't you get that sorted... like now?'

'God's sake Christine, get off your high horse. The poor creature must be on the verge of collapse from overuse. I'm just asking for a layman's opinion.'

'The hospital don't think so. They kicked me out for tiring her too much; I doubt they're going to look kindly on you dragging her in front of the cameras.'

'I didn't ask what the hospital thought.'

'Yeah, she'll be okay to do it. It will give her some degree of confidence that she's taking action to find her daughter, and that'll help her out more than "getting rest".' I mimicked a set of air quotes to add the required amount of hostility.

'Cool. She'll need you there again to call on so we look like we're offering enough support.'

'I don't work for you any more remember? Rena knows my number and she's free to call me for support when and if she needs it.'

'Ever known a parent go in front of the media and not need support before, during and afterward?'

I hated it when other people had a point. Especially when they were grinning at me like they were on their way to Oz to find a brain.

'I'll get in contact with her after you've told her the plan. If I contact her before it will just make it look like we're colluding.'

'We are.'

'You are. And you're ignoring the moral objections that I continue to make.'

'Good, good,' Erik continued as though I'd just agreed with his position wholeheartedly. One more notch on my disgruntled bedpost.

'And don't act like you know me if I'm there supporting Rena,' I answered back. 'I don't want it to look like I have any relationship with the police aside from my place of work.'

'You don't, Christine.' Erik responded as he walked away. 'You remind me frequently.'

I gave his back my middle finger. Always a wonderful refuge when the object concerned wasn't looking.

**

'What will they ask? What if I don't know what to say? What do I do then? I really don't know that I should be doing this. The nurses said it was a bad idea, and I'm starting to believe they're right.'

Rena had been moved out of ICU against all advice, and was sitting in a wheelchair in a quickly vacated patient's lounge waiting for her television appearance with all the anticipation of a Samoan to a dawn raid.

'The nurses said it was fine to go ahead with it as long as you felt comfortable. If you don't want to do it you can just say the word and I'll sort it out for you.' I put a hand on the back of Rena's hand, and felt her quick pulse vibrate through the back of her hand before she waved me off.

'I do want to do it. I do.' Rena turned her head toward me and I could see how her fear and worry were wearing creases into the contours of her face. She was starting to look her age. 'I just don't know if I can. What if I make it worse?'

'You're not going to make it worse Rena. You're just going to sit there and tell the public about Chloe and how much you want her to come home. You're going to answer the questions that you feel you can, and ignore the ones that you can't. Just shake your head and DSS Smith will make sure to move onto the next one. And if you want it to stop just tell him you can't go on and he'll stop it.'

Rena put her hand towards her mouth, and then quickly pulled it back into her lap, her mouth a moue of disgust. I guessed she was a nail biter from way back. Given her age the popular trick around at the time she was a child would've been to paint her nails with a bitter tasting formula. The trick lived on in her mannerism.

'Could you do it instead?' Rena asked turning her face full to mine, her eyes pleading. 'You're good at public speaking aren't you, I can tell. You'll do a much better job.'

'Look Rena, I can sit beside you if it makes you feel more comfortable. I can help out with questions that you've already told me the answer to, and field them where I can. But I can't sit there and tell them why Chloe is so special. I can't tell them what she does that makes you laugh, what she does that makes you proud. I can't explain why she's so important that everyone should stop what they're doing right now and make sure that they tell someone if they saw anything. Only her mother can do that. And you'll be able to do that Rena. Just focus on Chloe, and let me and DSS Smith support you through this and you'll be fine.'

Rena still didn't look convinced, but she nodded her head in agreement anyway. Her deep frown of worry would translate well onto the television news. As would her apparent nerves and fear. I hated myself for thinking of her in such clinical ways, but I couldn't stop assessing her level of pain and worry and ticking all the boxes that would make members of the public pay attention and do the things they needed to do to move this investigation forward.

Erik walked through the door without any of the courtesies you'd expect from a man of his position. Manners were on a one-way street flowing out from his centre. Rena jumped at the unexpected entrance; her nerves frayed by one more broken thread.

'Everything is set up for us to go ahead. We'll just need to transport you out to the station for the appearance, and then we'll have you back here as soon as we can.'

'I'm not sure I can do this?' Rena said with her voice rising up into a question.

'I know it's hard, and strange,' Erik replied. He walked over to Rena's chair and bent down in front of her to make sure he met her eyes on the same level. 'No one is ever prepared to do these appearances, but everybody manages to get through. This is the one most important thing you can do at this stage to help the investigation. Everyone who sees you tonight is going to see a mother in pain, separated from her daughter, and they're going to want to reach out and help you. And one of those people could have the information we need to find Chloe.'

He stood up again, but continued to look at her. 'You'll be able to do this, and you'll be able to answer the questions you need to, and you'll never regret making this appearance. Never.'

It always took me by surprise when Erik acted like a human being. He was so good at it that it was confusing he didn't channel the ability more often.

'Okay,' Rena said. Her voice was soft, but she cleared her throat and repeated it with more force. 'Okay. I'm ready.'

***

There was a long table with five chairs spaced behind it. A cluster of boom mikes were mounted to the bench; a group where Erik indicated he would sit, and still more in front of Rena's seat.

A hum of low-voiced conversation grew louder as more and more journalists pushed into the room. They jostled and rustled and altered their positions while trying to keep an eye on everyone else in the room at all times. Rena grasped my hand and held it to her chest. There was a slick layer of sweat on her forehead and a shake in her shoulders.

Erik moved to her side, and bent down so he could speak at her ear level. It was becoming more and more difficult to hear anything except the hive of the conference room.

'Once we're seated I'll wait a few minutes before talking. It will give them a chance to get some visuals of you before we start. Just relax, and if you start to feel uncomfortable looking at the cameras just turn and look at me instead. Block them out. If you need to call a halt at any time let me or Christine know and we'll stop.' He smiled, and the fine lines around his eyes curved up. It was odd to see him treat someone so well, although I knew just from the position he'd reached that he must know how.

We entered in a group, and I kept my shoulder in front of Rena's in an automatic protective gesture. Rena sat down on the very edge of the seat. She dropped my hand and her own snaked out to the bench in front of her and began to tap away. Her blond hair was listless against her scalp; her skin a dull shade of grey. I'd tried to persuade Rena to retain the IV that fed her fluid and medication. It could be transported into the room beside her without much issue, but she'd refused. I sympathised with her pride, and the demand it placed on her to look strong and able-bodied in front of the press. The pity being it was a time when the reverse would elicit a better response from the gathered crowd.

I also hoped the nurses back at the hospital ICU weren't going to catch the broadcast. I'd assured them that Rena's medical needs would continue to be met.

Still, at the rate Rena was improving she wouldn't head back there anyhow.

On the other side of Erik I recognised Allie, who I'd worked with briefly. She'd been in rotation through child crimes at the time, and I wondered how she'd managed to wrangle her way back into the role. Six months was the usual limit, with a maximum extension of another six. Maybe things had changed in the meantime though. It'd been years since I'd been involved with that part of the police force in any capacity. My consulting days were well and truly past no matter how much Erik wanted to pretend they weren't.

The noise level continued to climb as camera crews reviewed their footage and tried to make adjustments in the crush of the room.

'Could everyone be seated,' Erik stated rather than asked. His voice was low and quiet but it carried well within the confined space and even intense conversations were broken off to obey.

'Rena Sutherland has kindly agreed to join me at the briefing today. As she's recently been involved in an accident that involved serious injuries to her person we'll try to keep this as brief as possible. There will be some time for questions, but please understand that Mrs Sutherland will not be able to answer all queries that you have at this time.'

Hands across the floor raised simultaneously but Erik waved them back down again.

'First I'll give you a brief overview of the case to date, and invite Mrs Sutherland to make a statement regarding her daughter. Officer Woods will provide you with press-packs which contain a recent photograph of Chloe, descriptions of the clothing she was wearing on the day, the location, and the other known details relating to the last instances that Chloe Sutherland was seen. She'll also be available to you after this press-conference if you need to confirm any details,' he waved his hand towards the officer at the back of the room, and she nodded her head.

He cleared his throat.

'We were informed early this morning of the disappearance of Chloe Sutherland. She was last seen on Thursday, just after midday. She was dressed in a pale-pink sundress with a white collar, and black patent-leather shoes in a Mary-Jane style. Her hair is light blond and shoulder-length, but was pulled back in a pony-tail and tied with a pink ribbon at the time.

'There was a car accident which involved a red Mazda model 323 - licence plate AJG223 - which collided with a stationary vehicle, a yellow Suzuki Swift - licence plate CWS334. The accident was located in the car-park of the Northlands Shopping Centre next to the Main North Road and beside the Flying Mohicans Restaurant.

'We would like to hear from all witnesses to this accident. If you were in the vicinity of this accident and have not yet been contacted by the police, we ask that you call the Christchurch North police station or the Crimestoppers free-phone number.'

He paused for a moment and allowed the still photographers from the newspapers to take another series of shots. Rena jerked back from the flashbulbs, and turned to stare at Erik as he began to speak again.

'Chloe Sutherland is aged four years old. She's a very small girl and she's now been missing for four days. We need the urgent assistance of the public at this time to try to locate her and make sure that she is returned home to her mother.

'Officers have been out in force today to conduct an extensive search of the area Chloe was last seen. They've conducted house to house enquiries and will continue to do so over the coming days. They've distributed leaflets with Chloe's picture and details throughout the surrounding suburbs.

'Once again I stress that if you have any information that may help with this inquiry, no matter how insignificant it may seem, please don't hesitate to talk to an officer, to phone the station, or to phone the Crimestoppers number. We need to hear from you.

'I'll now pass over to Mrs Sutherland to say a few words.'

Rena grabbed my hand under the bench and squeezed it so tightly for a moment that I flinched. She released it and folded both her hands in front of her, quieting the relentless tap of her fingers.

'My daughter Chloe is precious to me and to my ex-husband Ash. We wish nothing but her safe return. She is a good girl. She's quiet, she's polite, and she doesn't ever talk back. She's very clean and tidy. She likes to read in her room and draw pictures and use her dustbuster to clean out the corners and hang all her clothes up in order of their colour and dress her teddy bear in the same matching outfit that she's wearing each day.'

Rena's breath ran out. She paused to try to inhale deeply. It didn't quite work. She got a breath half-hitched in and then stopped altogether. I lifted a hand to pat her on the back but she manoeuvred her body away before it could land. She breathed in again, and pressed her knuckles of each hand into each eye. A moment passed. She let her breath out and took her hands away to expose her face; still and composed.

'I need to know if you've seen my little girl. My little angel. If you have please call the police or call another emergency service or call me on my cell phone 027 35...'

Erik held out a hand to cut her off.

'Just call the police. Once again, the last time that Chloe has been seen was on Thursday just after lunch in the car park of the Northlands Mall in Papanui. If you have any recollection of seeing her or Mrs Sutherland at the mall on that day, or were a witness to the accident, please contact us as soon as possible. We have officers waiting to take your statement.'

Erik turned to check Rena was still holding up, then turned back to the throng of journalists. 'We'll take questions now. Ask only when I point to you.'

He pointed to a woman planted in the first row who was already standing to make sure that she was noticed.

'What about the ex-husband. Is it true that he didn't alert anybody that his daughter was in danger?'

'Mr Sutherland did not notify hospital staff of his daughter's disappearance as he believed that she was in the care of his mother-in-law at the time. We have had our colleagues in Australia interview him this morning, and we will also talk with him upon his return to New Zealand.'

'Did the driver of the car that hit you kidnap your daughter?'

Erik frowned at the question. He definitely hadn't pointed at the questioner. Clare Saunders. She was so loose with the facts that even online blogs hesitated to quote her. But of course she had a following.

'The man involved in the car accident is being held in custody, and has been since the time of the accident,' he answered, his voice firm.

'Mrs Sutherland, do you think your husband has kidnapped your daughter?' Saunders called out, again not following the rules.

Rena turned a shocked face towards this query. She appeared at once to be baffled and fully angered.

'Ash loves Chloe as much as I do. Of course he didn't take her.'

'But you're in the middle of a custody dispute.'

Rena shook as she answered. 'We have reached an amicable agreement with the help of the courts system to share custody of our daughter, and he would never do anything to jeopardise his relationship with Chloe, or our relationship post-divorce.'

Saunders opened her mouth, but this time Erik stepped in. 'We'll bring this interview to a close there, I think. We'll let you know when the next briefing will be, and we should have more to share with you at that point.'

There were groans of protest from the assembled crowd.

'I'm sure you can understand that it has been an extremely long and tiring day for Mrs Sutherland, and we need to make sure that we don't endanger her health any further.'

Erik shuffled a few pieces of paper together on the bench in front of him, and held them tightly as he stood. Considering he hadn't referred to them once throughout I gathered that they were a visual prop rather than a tool.

Rena's shoulders slumped as everyone left the room.

I turned to her and smiled to try to show that it had gone well. She tried to return the smile, but her eyelids began to spasm and then her body began to shake. Her body slumped to one side and slid off her chair to land heavily on the floor, her back raised in a spasm.

'Call an ambulance' I shouted at the officer standing in stunned stillness next to the door.

I moved the chairs and shoved the bench aside and then tried to angle Rena onto her side, into the recovery position. Her body continued to strain in the grip of the strong muscular contraction of a seizure.

I guess I was going to be told off back at ICU after all.

***

'Christine, are you heading back to the station? I can give you a lift.'

The offer was so odd coming out of Erik's mouth that I was immediately suspicious. But I was also tired. I'd been running around trying to empathise with people all day, with varying degrees of success, and I just wanted to get home, hoe an enormous serving of something filled with sugar and fat into my mouth – maybe with a green salad to make me feel better – and then fall into bed. Alone, if Gary's earlier text was to be believed.

'That would be great.'

'Good. I want to pick your brain about something.'

He caught the look trying to climb onto my face and put up his hand, 'nothing untoward. Just a general inquiry.'

I thought about refusing and organising my own way back to the station. First I would have to get out of the hospital. Since I'd grabbed a lift here this afternoon I'd have to call a taxi. To do that I'd have to use a payphone down in the lobby. To get there I'd have to walk past a lot of people who'd been rather concerned that the patient I'd assured them would not be any the worse for wear by taking part in a news conference had instead had the first of a series of seizures that meant her re-admittance, unconscious, to the ICU I'd hoped she would be well enough to stay out of. I'd have to go past them anyway, but it would be easier next to the six foot four guy who was officially in charge. I gave in and followed him down the hall, careful not to let him get more than a footstep ahead.

'You said that Mrs Sutherland had a mental illness in her past?' Erik questioned as soon as his car pulled out of the hospital and joined the flow of traffic across the city. After the earthquake the old ebb and flow of traffic had changed, and changed again as streets were rendered impassable, cleared, and then rendered impassable again due to the scale of the roadwork required to get Christchurch's infrastructure back in place. We slowed to a crawl and waited for a change of lights to lead us back into a mobile state.

'And you said that you wouldn't ask me anything untoward.'

'Just thinking aloud. Her statement to the press was slightly off, don't you think?'

Of course I thought that. Where parents could usually be expected to espouse on how cute their children were, how smart they were, how playful, how full of joy and oh-so-unique and amazing and a wonder to watch in everything they did, Rena had instead spoken of neatness and ordering of clothes and vacuuming. I doubt there was a single person in that room who thought that was normal.

'And then I wondered if that might have any relevance to her former or current mental state. And then I thought, "why wouldn't someone warn her not to talk about her daughter like that in front of the entire New Zealand media who love it so much when a cute little white girl goes missing because they can wholeheartedly get in behind the search and complain about how much society has collapsed in the last decade," and you know what Christine? I couldn't think of a reason. Did you two not get on or something?'

'I advised her and supported her as best I could. I didn't know that she was going to say any of those things. It's certainly not how she described her daughter to me. Anyway I'm only meant to be her support through this awful time; I'm not her bloody media consultant.'

Erik pulled the car over to the side of the road and turned to face me.

'Well you'd better start thinking like a media consultant. Ash Sutherland is arriving back into the country in,' he glanced at his watch, 'less than two hours, and then you're going to have two clients needing you. Two clients, and they're going to be under the most media scrutiny that anyone in this country of ours ever has to face. In the best case scenario that means that they can come across to the country like a genuinely grieving couple that want nothing more than their daughter to be found. In the worst then you'll be in charge of Lindy and Michael Chamberlain, and with the weirdness that just poured out of Mrs Sutherland's mouth I think you can easily guess which way that's heading.'

'Well thanks for your concern.'

He didn't respond to my sarcasm, and I sat in silence next to him for the next few minutes.

'Do you know a parolee named Martin Hinks?' I ventured when the station was almost within view.

Erik frowned. 'Why?'

'He was released from prison last week. He'd been in there for rape and murder of a girl. A young girl.'

'I know who he is. I meant why the interest?'

'I just wondered if he had been located back to this area. He was originally from Bishopdale after all.'

Erik pulled the car smoothly into his reserved park and pulled the handbrake on forcefully, making it jump.

'You can wonder all you like.'

'I've helped out you today. Would be nice if I could rely on a little bit of quid pro quo.'

'I didn't ask you to cross any lines that you weren't able to justify to yourself.'

'And what would you need to justify this to yourself?'

Erik grinned, then reached across my lap to open my car door. 'Nothing you can provide me with.'

I continued to sit, and Erik continued to stare at me levelly while I did so.

'Are you really not interested in Ash as a suspect?'

Erik laughed and shook his head. I guessed that

wasn't an indication of his position, just that I wasn't going to get it out of him. 'I'm sure you can find your own way from here,' he said pointedly.

I gave up and got out of the car to wind my way through the carpark to the far corner which was where my own vehicle was located. There was a steady hum of drunken chatter from the back garden of a pub that almost backed up to the park. The central strip may have been closed down but people still needed to drink. Even at nine o'clock on a Monday night.

I heard Erik back his car out of the park and take off north. So he really had just been giving me a lift back to the police station. I'd assumed it would only be because it was convenient, but since that now wasn't the case I paid more attention to his little pep talk.

If DSS Smith had felt it necessary to pull me aside for long enough to talk to me about my client's state of mind, then it must be important. I would definitely take some notice of what he thought. Tomorrow.

For now I was heading home and picking up something hot on the way so I could stuff it into my mouth and then fall asleep alone. Hooray for married life.

It took longer for me to collect the Chinese takeaway number 17 – otherwise known as Chicken Fried Rice with Cashews – than it did to swallow it and put away the empties in the outside rubbish bin. I don't know the value of not eating all day and then eating three to four serves of food all at one go, but I'm willing to bet that as a diet it's probably not going to end up in the next episode of fitness and health.

I lay down on the sofa to watch some TV, but when the end credits come up on a show I could've sworn only appeared on screen a few minutes before I took the hint and went to bed. I felt like I'd only just closed my eyes when I bolted upright in bed to the unmistakable sound of a burglar breaking into the front door.

I swung my arm out to my side in the forlorn hope that Gary had snuck into bed without me noticing. He hadn't. I felt down to the floor on my side to see what was close to hand, and gratefully curled my fingers around the universal remote. It felt like a threatening shape, and it was solid-plastic with four double A batteries heavy.

There was another scrape across the front door. I forced myself to get out of bed and pulled my saggy pyjama bottoms up so I wouldn't trip over the legs.

Should I turn on the lights? What if that scared them away? Well, that would be a good thing wouldn't it? But don't you want to beat them over the head with a remote for scaring the shit out of you while you phone the police to make sure they're locked away forever? I realised I wasn't moving and started to creep down the side of the stairs. Even with the lights off there was enough illumination from the moon and streetlights outside for me to see rather than feel my way.

Deep breath in. Deep exhale out. Deep breath in.

I tiptoed across the polished wooden floor, careful to avoid the squeaky board near to the landing, but horrified to discover that there were plenty more determined to make as much sound as they could.

There was the low muttering of a voice outside. Two burglars? Three? Then the scraping sound recommenced.

I stood beside the door, gathered all my anger and fear into a ball of energy and turned on the outside light just before I flipped the deadbolt off and heaved the door open, my weapon hand raised.

Gary gave a whimper as the light hit his drunk laden eyes, and then a grateful cheer as he walked carefully in through the opened door.

He shook his keys at me.

'Damn door key isn't working,' he announced, efficiently transposing all of the blame.

'Gary, that's the car key.' The thick rod he clasped in his fingers in no way resembled our thin multi-toothed front-door key.

'Exactly,' he stated with firm conviction and headed into the kitchen. I closed and re-deadbolted the door behind me and followed him through. I wondered how long he'd actually been working tonight, and how long he'd instead spent drinking. Possibly no overtime given the slump of his ankles and the shuffle of his gait.

'Gary you can't eat that! It's almost eleven o-clock for God's sake.'

I grabbed the raw steak out of his hand and found him a box of crackers to snack on instead.

'I'm going back to bed.'

I tried to say it with heavy emphasis. Tried to infuse it with meaning and hostility, but Gary just nodded and munched away.

I went back to bed, wide awake again. Only another few hours of fuming and it would be time to get up and go back to work.

CHAPTER FOUR

Entering the office the following day I felt as if I'd spent the night hopped up on speed rather than in a deep sleep. My eyes twitched repeatedly with the tired spasm of nerves, and my mouth was thick with dried saliva that three glasses of water hadn't managed to budge.

Gary had spent the night downstairs. Even his alcohol-addled brain was apparently astute enough to realise that I wouldn't welcome his company. He'd left his clothes conveniently draped over the sofa from where they were obviously meant to find their own way to the laundry. Since he had faith in this I left them there to see if it was true.

There was a missed call from the day before. It had been routed through to me rather than the first on-call because I'd dealt with the family previously. I passed the assignment back through to the co-ordinator. If Chloe's parents were both going to take up victim support they would be a pretty full-on job until their daughter was found, and then afterwards dependant on the condition she was found in. Usually I was only in touch with people who had already experienced the full crime or trauma and were living in the aftermath. It wasn't a similar basis on which to judge my current situation where it was still possible that no crime had even been committed.

There was a message on my answer phone from DSS Smith notifying me that they'd referred Ash Sutherland through to my services as well. Not unexpected. Ash Sutherland. I repeated the name a few times in my head to make sure I wouldn't snigger when he introduced himself aloud. I picked up the phone to call through.

Heading to the appointment at his home in Casebrook, I wondered at the tone in Erik's voice when he left the message. I doubted Rena's assertion that her husband wasn't a suspect in this case, and thought there was a good possibility I was about to meet with a man who'd spent most of his night explaining his actions in the smallest detail to the police.

From Ash's demeanour when I joined him at his house I would've guessed he'd flown in from Europe or the Arctic or some other country at the opposite side of the globe. Instead he'd made the enormous effort of flying back from Perth. Apparently flying took a lot out of him.

He was quiet at first; I'm used to that, especially with men. Although metrosexuals aren't usually part of my line-up. And then he opened his mouth.

'I understood that she was staying with Rena's mother. She'd talked about it a few months ago, though to be honest I didn't take a lot of notice at the time.' He ran a hand through overly long curly blond hair, and then ran it along his unshaven cheek. He yawned and didn't bother to stifle it with his hand. 'I just remember thinking that we'd both be away from Chloe at the same time and it might be hard for her. She's never been apart from both of us at the same time before.'

'When did you find out that she wasn't at her grandmother's?'

He shook his head and shrugged.

'I knew something was wrong when two officers turned up at my door this morning.' He shook his head again. 'I mean yesterday morning, and then dragged me down to the police station to answer some of their questions. They finally told me when I was at the station.'

'That must've been rough.'

'Yeah, you could say that. I thought they'd mixed me up with a drug dealer or something. And then they tell me something even worse. I wasn't at all prepared for that. And then I had to scramble to rearrange everything so I could come home, and then I have to deal with another set of interviews at another police station in another country.'

He squeezed his forehead with his fingers, creating vertical frown lines, and then relaxing. Frown. Relax.

'I've been helping Rena out with a few things. She had to do the television interview yesterday, and there may be more media briefings coming up. Has she been in contact with you?'

He snorted and shook his head. 'No. Rena hasn't been in contact with me.'

I hesitated before I asked the next question. There was something beneath the surface here, and I didn't know if it was because Rena was living in a fantasy land, or if I was wrong about the signals that Ash was giving off.

'At the press conference Rena gave the impression that you too were still close. Is that still the case?'

Ash sat forward in his chair and stuck his finger in my face. His hand shook, but not with anger. It was the caffeine jitters. My response was still the same. I flinched back.

'I don't know what business that is of yours. I don't even know why you're here. Someone suggested I seek support and the next thing I know you're sitting in my lounge, asking me questions. As if I hadn't had enough of that already.'

'I didn't mean to offend you Mr Sutherland. I was trying to ascertain your relationship to see whether you'd benefit from having contact with a different victim support volunteer. If you and Rena aren't on good terms then you probably don't want me in the middle.'

He sat back and rubbed his face briskly with his hands. He shrugged again.

'I can't stand the sight of her and she annoys the shit out of me, but I don't need to be kept in a separate box.

We spent long enough together when I thought she was barking mad for me not to care now. As long as everyone is focused on finding Chloe what annoys me about my ex-wife can go on hold.'

It was a more mature answer than I would've given him credit for, but on the other hand I'd met him less than an hour before and it sounded like he hadn't slept in about 36 times that at least. First impressions are so harsh I don't know why I rely on them, but they're hard little suckers to shake off once they're formed.

But then Ash promptly gave me reason.

'She always had a different routine for each day of the week, you know. She's like an OCD Gestapo agent. Rena can't do anything except in a set order. You were never allowed to leave any mess around the house.' He laughed briefly, but without much humour. 'It got worse after Chloe was born. At the end I felt like she spent her whole day following me around with a damp sponge.' He shook his head, then straightened his shoulders. 'That was why I wanted Chloe to live with me, why I wanted primary custody. It drove me crazy and I was always a regularly tidy guy. Not gay tidy you know, but not lazy or dirty or anything. I don't know what Chloe's going to turn out like if she's exposed to any more of that. She's not allowed to play. She's not allowed to leave anything anywhere. She's forced to eat over the sink in the kitchen - can you imagine that? She's four years old and her mother feeds her in a high chair over the sink. And then she comes to my place and she doesn't know how to feed herself. I have to give her finger food because I don't have enough time with her to teach her how to eat with a knife and a fork. And even if I did, she'd not be allowed to do that at Rena's place. She'd be fed instead with a special spoon on Wednesday, and a special knife and fork on Thursday, and it's always 150g of meat, and 2 cups of vegetables and ½ cup of potatoes or rice or pasta because that's how you're meant to portion your meals and if you don't portion them that way then something terrible is going to happen, and she doesn't ever notice that the terrible thing is all the shit she does.'

Ash ran his hand over his face again, and rubbed his

knuckle into his eye.

'What day was it?'

'What day was what?' I asked, not following.

'What day was the car crash?'

'It was on Thursday. Around midday I think.'

'Right. Well Thursday was the day that she went grocery shopping in the morning, usually as soon as the supermarket opened because otherwise there were a whole lot of people and Rena wasn't fond of people. They make the world too dirty, you see. So she'd finish up there by 6:45 am at the latest, because she only ever purchases the same items, but she has to read the labels each time otherwise they might not contain the right ingredients and if they don't contain the right ingredients then something terrible is going to happen.

'Once she gets back home she has to put everything away in the refrigerator, then the freezer, then the cupboards, and they have to be put away in the right order because otherwise...' he let me fill in the gap.

'She then has to go out and fill up the car at the petrol station. She has to do that every day – it always has to be full. That's a relatively new one – from the earthquakes. She saw the lines of traffic at the service stations in February and freaked out. So now she goes and fills up the car every single day.

'She then has to go to a specialised car cleaning outfit on the Main North Road. Service stations are dirty places so the car has to be washed every day after filling up. Then she'll head to the lingerie shop in Northlands Mall. She has to park in the right spot outside though, her spot, otherwise something terrible will happen. She'll circle around the mall for hours until her park comes free, Chloe in the back trying to be whisper quiet so she doesn't upset her Mummy.'

'Once she's in her special car park she'll then go into Personal Things and refresh her stocks of underwear for herself and Chloe. She can't wear the same piece of underwear twice because it's dirty. She goes there because it's cheap – if she went to a normal price store she'd be broke by now.'

'Then she'll get in the car and go back to the

supermarket to pick up vegetables and fruit for lunch, or tea if she had trouble getting her park. She can't keep vegetables or fruit in the house overnight because it would spoil and then she'd be eating rotten food, so she has to shop for it daily, and only ever just before a meal otherwise it will start to decay before she can eat it.'

He trailed off, staring into space, and I looked down at the table for a few moments. It sounded like a nightmare.

'Was Rena under anyone's care for her condition?'

Ash shook his head. 'She refused to see anyone because she thought they'd stop her routines. And if they stopped her routines...'

I just nodded.

'What about Chloe? Is she enrolled in day-care or pre-school anywhere?'

Ash shook his head. 'That wouldn't be safe for her. She's barely been exposed to anyone her own age. That's why I've been trying to get custody, but then the judge decided on joint so I'm back to square one, and only seeing her on weekends.

'I've tried taking her to parks and playgrounds and children's centres so she can get to know some other kids, but it's hard to watch her. She doesn't understand how to play, and if I get on the swings or merry-go-rounds to show her she still won't join in. Rena's ruining her. She's ruining my daughter, and the courts decided to just let it keep happening because it's so important that little girls get full access to their mummies.'

His face twisted with frustration and anger. I kept silent. No use pointing out that joint custody could follow any arrangement the parent's agreed upon – it didn't have to be father's relegated to the weekend. But maybe Ash liked having the excuse that he'd tried rather than he liked the idea of actually taking advantage of the joint idea behind joint custody.

There was a knock on the door. Then another.

Ash's face looked puzzled, then he moved over to open it.

'Rena. What the hell are you doing here? I thought you were in hospital.'

I stood up and moved over to the door, astonished. There was no way they should've discharged her.

Rena wasn't standing at the door so much as letting the walls of the house prop her there. She looked a fraction better than she had the previous night – although amid all the yelling and admonishments from hospital staff it was hard to picture her in the scene – but was still unsteady on her feet.

'Are you okay, Rena? Did the hospital discharge you?'

She shook her head, and the motion repeated itself throughout her whole body.

'I had to ask them to let me go. I signed about a hundred different forms,' she broke off to yawn, her mouth stretching her whole face into disfiguration, before she resumed. 'The doctors kept telling me it was a bad idea, but they didn't have me hooked up to anything at the time so I just kept saying I'd walk out anyway so they arranged for me to go.'

'What are you doing here?' Ash said. His tone of voice was not welcoming, but Rena didn't even look like she noticed. I wondered how bad their marriage had been that he could be rude without even jolting her in the slightest.

'I thought it would be easier on everyone if they just had one point of contact for us. And there's not enough room in my place – you know that.' As Ash continued to stare at her with horror, Rena faltered, but then rallied again. 'And since I knew you wouldn't want to be traipsing back and forth to the hospital all the time I thought you'd appreciate it too. What do you think?' she asked, turning to me instead.

'I think we should get you inside and onto a couch before we continue this discussion. You look exhausted.'

I grabbed her arm, and bullied Ash aside from the door so I could escort Rena in. After listening to his diatribe against her a few minutes earlier I could understand his reluctance, but that didn't mean she should be allowed to collapse.

'Do you need a glass of water or something?'

'How about I make the offers in my own home?' Ash said as he thumped the front door closed behind him.

'I'm fine, thank you. Just need to catch my breath.'

I sat with care on the edge of the sofa. I would've felt like a spare wheel, but it was so clear that Ash's hostility was directed in just one place that I got off lightly.

'Ash, you were just saying earlier that you and Rena should put aside any animosity until Chloe was found safe and well. It looks like you're both on the same wavelength.'

Rena shot a grateful look in my direction, and Ash sighed and sat down on his chair, a clear indication he was relenting.

'Yes, I was. Welcome home Rena.'

Rena ignored his sarcasm and smiled. Almost in triumph.

***

I left the Sutherland's in each other's company a short time later and drove back to the station. My office phone was lit up – a bad sign that I was determined to ignore. I'd left an answer message with the next point of contact for victim support. If the phone-ins couldn't follow directions they were past my help anyway.

My mobile phone buzzed in my pocket and I pulled it out, hoping that Gary might have phoned in to apologise for last night. If he remembered last night.

No such luck.

'Hi Kendra. How're you doing?'

'Christine? I'm good. Terry's not. Could you drop by?'

I looked at the well-lit phone, and then looked out the office door to see Erik peer through the gap.

'Sure I can. Where are you?'

'At hers.'

'I'm right on my way. Be there in five.'

Erik held up his hand, wait. I shook my head and repeated my statement.

'I have to go Erik. It's an emergency.'

'We need to talk.'

'You can walk me to my car,' I said as I swept by him.

'I wanted to check your thoughts on Ash Sutherland.'

I turned to face him. 'No. I'm not playing this game

anymore. You want to find out something about Ash ask him yourself.'

He'd peeled off by the time I got to my car. I wasn't quite right on the timing. There were road works on the Main North Road that meant I faced a choice of being held up or re-directed. I chose re-directed and spent the extra two minutes wondering if I'd made the right decision.

'Hey,' Kendra said. She was waiting outside the house as I pulled into the driveway.

'Hey yourself. What's up?'

'She's freaked out about Martin. Thinks she saw him at the mall this morning. Assumes he was waiting for little girls to torture.'

I stopped mid-stride. 'Do you think it was him?'

Kendra shrugged. 'Could be. Without knowing where he's been deposited it's hard to know how likely.'

I knocked on the door, but Kendra just pushed me aside and bowled right in. 'Terry. Your shrink's here.'

'Did she tell you? I saw him walking around the mall like he had every right to be there. There's a crèche in that mall. He could've taken one right then and there.'

'Did you approach him?'

'He walked off too quick for me to follow. He was half-way across the food court before I even twigged it was him.'

'Are you sure it was.'

Terry's eyes were daggers.

'I see his face every night before I go to sleep. Some night's that all I look at instead of sleeping. I think I'm experienced enough with his face to know when I see him alright.'

'They shouldn't allow people like that back near malls and stuff, should they?' chimed in Ilene as she walked through the door. 'There's about twelve different schools in this area. Don't they have rules about that sort of stuff?'

'If he's actually in the area. He may just have access to a car,' I replied. 'There'll be restrictions on how close he can go to certain areas I suppose, but I don't know the details.'

'Maybe we should go back there. How long since you've seen him Terry?'

Terry looked down at her watch. 'Maybe an hour.'

'Some people hang around malls for far longer than that, don't they?' said Ilene. 'Let's go back there. See if we can catch up with him again.'

'I don't think that's a good idea,' I interjected. 'What are you going to do if we do see him again? Unless he's making a parole violation we can't do anything.'

'Well what would one be? We could say we saw him doing that.'

'Ilene I'm not going to lie to the police. I have to work next to them every day you know.'

'Not lie. Just stretch out the truth.'

'Terry love, are you okay?'

Ilene and I turned to see Kendra helping Terry to a seat in the dining room. Her face had drained pale.

'Do you want me to call Jacob for you, Terry? He could come and sit with you.'

'No. I don't want him here. I haven't told him about the release anyway so he won't know what you're talking about.'

I caught Kendra's eye but she just shrugged. Terry didn't interact with her oldest child much anymore, but I would've thought she might have passed on this information.

'What do you want to do?' I asked.

'I want to find out where he's staying and then go around and strangle him. That's what I'd like to do.'

'You know we'd alibi you up,' Ilene said with enthusiasm, placing her hand on Terry's shoulder.

'We're not going to let you do anything stupid,' I said with as much force as I could muster. 'I think it's a much better idea that we sit here until you're feeling calmer, and then we talk through a strategy of what to do if you do ever encounter him again. If Martin has been released around here then there's a chance you could bang into him again, you know.'

'I thought they didn't allow criminals back near their victims?' Ilene said with indignation. 'Why should Terry have to come up with strategies? He should be the one to be coming up with ideas of what to do if I ever catch sight of him around here.'

Martin wouldn't have felt safe if he'd heard the intonation that Ilene gave her speech.

'I could carry a knife,' Terry said, her voice soft with menace. 'That way I'd be ready for him.'

'You said he was halfway across the room before you even recognised him,' I pointed out. 'Not much good a knife'll do you. And if you're caught with one you're going to be in a lot of trouble. Not to mention the damage it'll do to the lining of your jacket.'

Kendra stared at me in disbelief for a second then gave a bark of laughter.

'She could keep it in her purse.'

'Even worse,' Terry contributed. 'Imagine stabbing myself every time I go to get out my wallet.'

'We'll know what's going on when you refuse to pay for lunch in future then.'

'Yeah, either that or I can't fit in my wallet and my gun.'

'If you're going to upgrade your hardware don't settle for a handgun. You want to go the whole hog. Get a grenade.'

'A pocket-sized rocket launcher.'

'A carry-case sized nuclear warhead.'

'A vial of small-pox.'

Terry started to laugh and we joined in with her. Full-on revenge plans initiated.

***

I tidied up a few loose ends back in the office, and then headed out the door for lunch. I'd been eating so many takeaways lately that I considered it was time to pick up a salad or slaw instead of the usual, but the idea didn't take root and grow the way I needed to, and there was a quarter pack of chicken calling out to me.

I'd successfully avoided Erik since returning from Terry's place. It had been easy, so I figure he was probably trying to do the same from his end.

Rena called to talk about the media that was outside

her and Ash's house, and what they should do about them, so I talked her through the protocol of staying away from windows and doors, and only going outside if you had something to say. If the media scrum continued they'd be eating a diet similar to mine shortly.

There was paperwork to be filed for earlier cases, and also I'd avoided doing the bi-annual coursework I needed to maintain for so long that they now appeared in bold red on my to-do list, but I wasn't feeling it today. I stayed out to lunch for an extra fifteen minutes – the perks of an unpaid volunteer – and then sloped back to the station to push paper around until I felt it was a reasonable time to stop.

My phone vibrated as I neared my desk, and I reached to answer it at the same time I saw my desk phone was lit up with messages again.

'Christine – it's Rena here.'

'Hi Rena, how're you coping?'

'Can you come around to the house?'

'Of course. I'll just tidy up a few things and be there in an hour.'

'Could you make it any sooner than that?'

Rena's voice had a tone I knew well. It was the voice of someone who always knew they weren't important enough to demand things, but really needed something anyway that they were too scared to ask.

'I'll come out now. Is there anything wrong?' I bit my tongue in frustration, of course there was. 'Anything specific?'

'I'll wait until you're here if you don't mind?' Her voice was quiet and pleading and I felt like a monster for even asking her to explain.

'I'll be there as soon as I can.'

There were a few journalists hanging around outside, and they all jerked to attention as my car pulled into the driveway and surrounded my vehicle.

I banged the door open as hard as I could while they nimbly danced out of harm's way, then shielded my face with one hand as I strode to the entrance.

It opened wide before I had to knock and I stepped in, grateful to be out of the milieu of media.

'Thank you for coming so quickly,' Rena said as she limped through to the couch. 'I really appreciate it.'

'What's the matter? What can I do to help?'

Rena looked around her for a moment, as though she'd misplaced the information she needed to continue, but then shook herself and patted the couch next to her.

I sat down, careful not to put my weight too close to hers so Rena wouldn't be pulled to the side, but there was still no information forthcoming.

'Was there something specific you needed me to do?'

She shook her head, and then nodded.

'What is it? What can I help with?'

Rena looked around the room again. Her fingers started to tap out their favourite pattern on the worn beige leather of the couch. I started to grow frustrated. Was I meant to guess?

'Is Ash sleeping?' I asked as I realised that I couldn't hear him in the house. It was a small bungalow so there wasn't very far he could go.

'No,' Rena replied, without adding any further information.

'Rena, unless you tell me what's wrong, or give me a signal of what's happening with you, I can't help you.'

She turned back to me again. 'You remember at the television thing. Someone asked me if Ash could be involved.'

I looked around to check that Ash wasn't hovering by a doorway listening, and I nodded. I remembered.

'I said he wouldn't do that to me or to Chloe.'

'Yes Rena. I remember. You defended him very well.'

She nodded. 'I did, didn't I?'

I waited again as her face seemed to turn off all lines of thought. Was it wrong to poke an injured mother with a missing child in order to get information out of her?

'He's gone.'

I looked around the room again, as though that would give me any further information.

'Gone where?'

Rena looked me in the eye again, and I saw for the first time that she wasn't speechless because she was shy, or quiet, or unused to the attention. She was speechless with pure, venomous fury.

'You mean he's really gone?' I started in surprise. 'When? When did he leave?'

'Last night,' Rena choked out. Her face began to turn red and her fingers tapped faster and faster.

'He said he was popping out to get a few extra supplies for his "unexpected house guest," ' she spat the words out. 'I've been sitting here waiting for him to get back ever since. But he's not coming back. He's not coming back, is he?'

My tongue wanted to spit out "why the fuck didn't you tell me when you called earlier" but I bit down hard and willed it into silence.

'Have you told anyone else this, Rena?'

She shook her head.

'Are you okay if I call the police and let them know?'

She stared at me with wild eyes, and then fear jerked her head back against the couch behind her.

'They'll think I should've called earlier, won't they? They'll blame me for it.'

'Rena, if Ash has taken Chloe. If he's arranged for her to be picked up and he's gone to get her now then the police are going to blame nobody but him. If that is what he's done then you need to tell them immediately. They can shut down routes out of the country, but only if they know what's going on.'

'I told everyone that he had nothing to do with it. And now he's buggered off. He's probably got her in his arms right now, and I've got nothing. He's left me with nothing!'

I glanced nervously at the window to the side. Rena's voice was now so loud I expected the media to be crowding shadows against the wall, but there was nothing there.

'Do you want to make the call, or would you prefer me to?' I asked instead of trying to assuage her anger and guilt. She would have time enough to sort that out for herself in the future.

'You do it. I can't trust myself.'

I made the call.

CHAPTER FIVE

Ilene's Story

After living with Brian for three years it was hard to remember why I thought he'd be a good man to marry.

At night he would sit down next to me on the couch, and I'd spend the next few hours inching away. My teeth would grind together harder with every stupid flaccid word that emitted from his slack mouth - a mouth I used to look forward to kissing, how did I ever think that was a good idea?

I would remind him to take out the rubbish on Friday mornings, and then take it out myself when it looked like he'd miss the six o'clock deadline.

I would ask him to balance the chequebook, and then I'd do it myself when the account went into overdraft.

I would remind him to put the oven on to 180ºC when he got in from work so the casserole I'd spent hours preparing when he "didn't know what I feel like for dinner tomorrow" would be nice and cooked through by the time I got in from my overtime shift at work. Of course I understood when he put it onto 220ºC instead because "it would cook faster". Even though I wasn't going to change the time I came home so it didn't really need to be cooked faster. Even though when the oven started to smoke the only action he took was to turn it off and open a window.

I would ask his opinion, ask for a decision, ask for any goddamn help with any adult task you could expect a couple to have to perform, and I would get silence or a shrug or a promise to do it later that I knew he'd never keep.

Every time he told me he'd do something and didn't I could feel a gap growing between us. Every time he left it up to me to make a decision I would move a squirm further down the couch.

I made up my mind to leave. Another decision he'd left it up to me to make. I'd made up my mind to leave but I'd put if off because I knew it was going to be hard, and I knew my parents were going to be disappointed with me, and I knew that money would be tight and the acrimony would be long.

I'd made up my mind to leave and then I found out that I was pregnant.

Stupid, isn't it? I don't think we'd touched each other more than half a dozen times in the last eighteen months, but when I knew that it was only a matter of time until I never had to see, feel, touch him again I felt far more inclined to do so.

Yes, stupid.

I thought for a time that I'd just get rid of the problem, just make it go away. I could continue to make plans for my own life, continue to make plans to leave, to get away, to move on. And then I realised that I could do that anyway. I didn't need to stay with a husband I hated in order to keep a child I'd love. I could do both things.

I told my husband about the baby at the same time that I told him I wanted a divorce. He didn't seem bothered about either. I moved out and I started to save every penny I could because the last thing I wanted was to take a penny from that worthless, useless man.

That dream died after a short illness.

When Angie was born she was the perfect baby. Sweet, round and cuddly. She was smiling from the first day - something that others insisted was due to gas but I knew better - and she loved to be held and to be fed and to sleep, thank god she loved to sleep.

I would put her down and she would smile and gurgle and then she would put her head to one side and she would be gone. Beautiful, good, a perfect baby.

Then one night that all changed. She started to cry and she wouldn't stop. All the inner one-upmanship that came with having the perfect baby disappeared in less than eight hours of crying. I couldn't work out what was wrong so I took her, fearful and tearful, to the emergency room so they could fix whatever was wrong.

But they couldn't find anything wrong. They complimented me on my perfect, sweet baby, and when she slept for ten minutes straight with no fever and no rash and no breathing trouble they handed her to me to take home.

I had been working from home; I had done some data-entry during the day so that my bills wouldn't stack up. I had done that when I had a quiet good baby. I couldn't with the noise monster that she'd suddenly turned into. The crying continued and I was too tired, and too wound up, for my fingers to work on a keyboard.

So there was no money coming in and the nest-egg I'd stored up to ward off any unexpected events dipped lower and lower and then was gone.

My ex-husband, who had not been particularly interested in anything Angie and I had done up to this point, suddenly turned into a loving supportive father. I hated it. I hated it when I dropped Angie off for her court-appointed visitation, crying her little head off, and I'd hand her across and she'd stop and start smiling up at her daddy.

I hated that I had to rely on his money in order to get through my day to day life. That I was on a benefit I didn't mind, but that part of it was made up of his support I hated.

And then he fought me for custody.

It came out of nowhere; I thought that the first letter was some kind of joke or trick or prank. But then he followed through and court dates were set and mediation was failed and everything was spinning out of control.

If he got primary custody of my sweet, loud, baby girl then I'd have to go around to his house to pick her up for visitation. I'd be the one wondering what she was up to half the time and I wandered about my empty house. I thought every time she cried I would've given anything to be free of her and able to go back to work with adult humans, but when the chance presented itself I realised I would give anything not to.

I fought hard against the claims. I submitted how he hadn't visited her regularly until she was three months old. How he hadn't been interested in my pregnancy, or offered to help out with her birth, or provided equipment for her baby room, or knitted her pretty little bonnets and cardigans to dress her noisy little body.

But he came back with how I'd obstructed him from being involved. How I'd changed classes so he couldn't be involved in the birth. How he'd applied for visitation and been granted it, but I hadn't ever been home when he came to pick up his daughter. How until I needed money I had forcefully kept her out of his life.

And then he started telling the court about the bruises that he had graphic photos of and the visits to the emergency department and how he thought it was in the child's best interest to be placed with him as primary custodian and I should only be allowed supervised visitation if I wanted to see Angie at all.

The very thought was horrific. I wept and I explained and I negotiated and I bargained and I argued and it finally seemed as those the case may be going my way; that I may be able to keep hold of her.

And then my ex-husband disappeared.

He didn't turn up at the court. I've never seen him again.

He took my daughter, my daughter, and I'll never stop searching until I find her again.

CHAPTER SIX

I left Rena in the tender clutches of the police and went back to the office. My co-worker Stevie was off somewhere helping her own contacts, and only the paperwork awaited my attention. First I phoned through to Nurse Maude to arrange a care-worker for Rena. With Ash out of the house she'd need some assistance, and she was still against the idea of returning to hospital. I arranged a visit at her home as she'd be kicked out of Ash's by the police search if nothing else, and then I phoned through to the regional office to let them know my time would be opening up again in future - crime solved; closure on its way. Rena still had my number if she needed help later, but hopefully the police would be able to reunite her with Chloe, and lock Ash up somewhere he would find out firsthand what it was like to be separated from a loved one.

I worked on for another few hours. Erik rushed in at one stage, then out again giving me a curt nod of recognition, but that was the most excitement I could see through my door.

When I picked up my mobile phone I realised it had turned itself off during the day. Usually I had it turned up enough so a series of beeps would alert me that it was time to either switch the battery or attach the charger, but I must have set it to silent as well after Rena's call through. Great service - that's what I'm known for.

It could wait until I got home in any case. I was now officially off duty. Having a dead phone was really a benefit to that end.

I couldn't be assed going home, eating alone, and then watching Gary come in from another session of "working late" so I turned off and headed toward the nearest Hoyts. A movie offered two hours of calming darkness, and came complete with popcorn. As I sat down in my seat with a giant tub - I always ignored urban legends about rats and theatres just for these occasions - I realised that I should be doing this sort of thing more often. Maybe next time I could even get extravagantly social and invite the girls along. Terry could point torchlight down the aisles trying to locate paedophiles and Ilene could alert us to the global conspiracy theories of the large movie companies. An excellent idea. On the other hand, maybe I could come alone again.

As I turned into my street my hope of finding my home in darkness was dispelled. The bloody thing was lit up like a Christmas tree.

Did Gary really have to turn on every light in the house? Maybe there was a true link to the phrase blind drunk that I'd missed out on in my long forgotten binge-drinking youth.

I opened the front door as quietly as I could. If Gary was sleeping it off already I had no wish to wake him up. I could sleep through his repeated retching but there was no way I'd fall asleep to it; even given how tired I felt.

The two outside lights were on, and I turned them off as soon as I gently closed the front door. What had he been planning to do? Sit outside in the light drizzle for some entertainment?

'Christine? Christine!'

I closed my eyes and leaned my forehead against the welcome cold of the wall. The jacquard pattern was rough against my skin. What would happen if I just walked quietly back out? Surely no one would notice if I spent one night sleeping at the station. It could be the cure for my exhaustion. I reluctantly pushed the idea aside and walked through into the lounge.

Gary had his shirt off, the top button of his pants unbuttoned, and his shoes and socks were nowhere to be seen. There was a clammy sheen to his skin; alcohol sweat compounded over the last few days. I hoped this wasn't meant to be a turn-on.

'It's been a long day at the office for you honey. What choo been doing?'

Gary made a baby-face that I didn't have the time for. I pulled my light jacket off and tossed it over the back of the chair closest to the door.

'There's a missing girl. The Dad's just disappeared so he's probably run off with him. The Mum's been in hospital and only just came out of a coma, so that was a nice surprise for her.'

Gary's face froze. Missing children still cut too close to the bone.

'Oh no. A little girl or boy?'

I felt like just saying yes and leaving the room. But Gary probably wouldn't get the play on words, and then he'd just follow me until he got an answer. He could be a tenacious drunk.

'A little girl aged four. Her name's Chloe.'

'I saw that one on the news. It didn't say anything about her Dad taking her.'

'We didn't know at the time. But he's gone missing...'

'At least she's with someone who loves her. At least she's got that.' Easy tears of self-pity started to roll down Gary's face, and I my lip curl; an involuntary reaction like when my doctor hits my knee with a hammer and my foot bounces. I didn't understand how I could miss my husband so much when I didn't see him, and yet hate him when I did.

I walked through into the kitchen and grabbed a few cheese-slices out of the fridge. The pop-corn had been great, apart from the husks still stuck in various teeth, but I needed some protein and it was all that we had. I pulled off the individual plastic wrap, piled the three slices on top of each other, folded them over and ate them in four bites.

I looked at the clock over the counter. It was almost nine o-clock. Far too late to eat, but a reasonable time to go to bed.

'Where're you going?'

I ignored him and carried on up the stairs.

'I said where're you going? I thought we could sit on the couch and watch a little telly, have a little drink. You need it after the day you've had.'

'I don't need a drink Gary. That's you remember?'

He flinched back against the insult, and I felt a stab of guilt that just made me angrier.

'I'm tired, I've had a long day, and all I want to do is go to bed.'

'Don't you want some company honey? I've had a hard day too.'

I stopped and looked down at him. Gary worked - when he felt like it - at a real estate agency. Houses in Christchurch didn't need any effort to sell or to rent at the moment, no matter what the price. Even the recent change to low-deposit lending hadn't put much of a damper on the system. He used to be a lawyer. He used to have an actual hard job. He used to have difficult clients, and investigations to find out what the truth was, or might be if framed correctly in front of a jury.

'What's been so hard Gary? Did you run out of breath mints right before you met up with a buyer?'

He looked aghast. The jibe was nothing serious. I'd definitely said far harsher things lately without him even taking notice. I sat down on the stairs with shock as my mind clicked through options and finally settled on the date with alarm bells ringing.

Shit!

I'd completely forgotten.

I'd ask myself what the hell kind of mother I was, but to face the truth I'd done worse things than forget my own daughter's birthday. Far worse things.

No wonder Gary was a psychological mess when I couldn't even remember something this simple.

Guilt ate its way into my gut, and a spasm made me regret eating the cheese. And the popcorn. And whatever else I'd shoved mindlessly in there today.

Bile coated the back of my throat but I choked it back.

'Gary, I'm sorry. I just... It was really full-on at work today. And this little girl's case - it's been so weird and hard and awful. I'm sorry - I just forgot.'

But I was speaking to his back as he walked away. Gary left the house and I double-stepped back down the stairs to make sure he wasn't going to drive away in his condition. But it looked like that was beyond him.

He lay, curled in a ball on the front lawn, his shoulders shaking. A thought of gratitude flitted through my head that at least I'd turned the lights off so the neighbours wouldn't see. Followed quick on its heels by the thought that there was a ring in hell reserved for people like me.

I left my husband crying on the lawn and went to bed with another three hours remaining of what should have been my daughter's fourteenth birthday.

***

I finally got around to charging up my cell-phone the next day. There was a string of ever more incoherent messages from Gary, and nothing else. He'd left by the time I went downstairs. He'd also taken my car rather than go to the bother of moving it to get his own out. I had another thought and went to check the fuel gauge of his vehicle. Yep. I'd need to fill it up on the way into the station.

There was no hurry so I didn't. It was after ten by the time I pulled into my lot, and I ambled rather than strode into the office.

'Hi Christine. How're you doing?'

Stevie was a flurry of activity at her desk. Shuffling papers, and then a rush of typing, then more shuffling.

I sat down and stared at my screen. After a minute or two I turned it on.

'Good. Fine.'

Stevie nodded eagerly, but seeing I didn't add anything more she tried a bit of unsubtle prompting.

'I saw your case took a bit of a turn yesterday.'

'Yes.'

'It must make it hard on Rena to know her husband was involved.'

I frowned at my screen. 'I didn't know they'd released those details.'

When an answer wasn't immediately forthcoming I turned to see that Stevie's cheeks had flushed, and she was no longer interested in catching my eye.

'No. Oh well, I must have overheard something out there,' she jerked her head towards the station proper.

'Right. Well I'm hoping that she'll soon have her daughter back safe and sound.'

Stevie made some sort of agreeable noise, but I wasn't really concentrating. I was thinking of Gary and me and wondering what the hell I should be doing as it certainly wasn't working out any more.

I had a referral first up. But when I phoned through the client's had changed their mind. Some more family had turned up and they didn't need anyone else involved. I reminded them that they could always call through if they changed their mind and then hung up.

I stared out at the station rooms, and wondered if I should continue on with my job any more than I should continue on with Gary. Maybe things would fall into place if I just upped stakes and left everything behind. Started fresh. The idea both appealed and appalled me. Leave everything behind - big tick. Start anew - God no. I had enough trouble keeping my sad little life chugging along now - I wouldn't have the strength to start from scratch.

My mobile rang chasing all my thoughts away.

Number unknown.

'Hi - Christine speaking.'

There was a long silence on the other end. I held fast. Sometimes it was a new client making their mind up on the other end of the line, and I'd learned not to demand an answer in a reasonable time-frame. When people were in crisis reasonable needed to be stretched.

'I'm here if you need to talk,' I prompted.

'Christine?'

I didn't recognise the voice, and it was so faint that I pumped the volume up as high as it could go.

'Yes, you're speaking with Christine. How can I help?'

'Christine. It's Ash. I need help.'

I stood up and ran to the door.

'Ash, where are you? How can I help?'

I saw Erik as he stepped into his office and firmly closed the door. It meant he didn't want to be disturbed. I wrenched it open.

'I don't know where I am. I'm hurt. Bad. I think I'm dying.'

I grabbed a pen and paper from Erik's desk while ignoring his infuriated face and wrote down ASH in big letters. I also pointed at the phone in case he'd misunderstood.

'Where are you?'

'I don't know,' Ash repeated. His voice faded in and out through heavy static. Wherever he was the reception was terrible.

A man stepped through behind me; I hadn't even heard Erik call through for him. He passed me a sheet and pointed.

'Ash. What type of phone are you calling me on?'

The heavy static drowned his voice out, and then it came back on a wave of clarity. 'An iPhone.'

'What's the number?'

Ash read out the number while I wrote it down. The man pointed to another line.

'Ash can you tell me your apple ID and password. I'll try to trace your phone from there.'

I wrote it down and the man hurried away. Erik took my arm and swept me through the station out to a waiting car.

'Ash, are you still there.'

Another rush of static and then the words, '... here.'

'I'm going to try to locate your phone and I'll drive to where the signal's coming from. Can you describe what's around you?'

'We've got a trace,' came a voice from the backseat, and Erik started the vehicle and we set off.

'... the police,' came through the phone faintly.

'What was that, Ash?'

'Don't call the police.'

***

Once Ash had been located I was unceremoniously dispatched away from the scene. Birdlings Flat. There was gorse in a field - the bright yellow flowers in stark contrast to the spiked green branches - but little else.

Although I was expected to deal with Ash's injuries, as soon as more help arrived I was placed in a car and driven straight back to the station.

You're welcome. No - don't mention it.

Stevie returned and rather than face another interrogation I decided to skip out for the day. Bugger it.

The day was turning out to be quite beautiful. There was a smattering of small cumulus clouds on the horizon; their clean white puffs make the skyline look like a cartoon. The sun was starting to pack some heat. It would be another couple of months until summer really began to dig its teeth in, but it was still nice to feel it trying.

I called through to Kendra to see if she was up for a morning skive-off, but she wasn't answering. I didn't want to go home, and I didn't feel like being with anyone else so I just drove around for a while and then parked the car and let the sun shine down on me.

Chloe hadn't been there. Ash was a bloody mess in a field in the middle of nowhere, and his daughter was not there with him.

I didn't know what it meant. I wondered if Rena had been informed of what had just happened. I wondered if I should call and let her know. I figured that since I'd been chucked out of the way as soon as was possible I'd probably be better off letting the police tell her in their own good time.

When my mobile rang I was happy to see that it was Kendra. I didn't need any further unknown numbers making an appearance.

'What's up?'

'Christine. Would you be able to pop round?'

'Sure. What's the problem?'

'I'll tell you when you get here.' There was the muffled sound of a hand being placed over a receiver, and then

Kendra's voice came back on the line. 'It might be urgent, love. Can you come over quickly?'

***

I wasn't that surprised to see Terry sitting at Kendra's dining table; eyes red from crying. I was surprised to see Jacob sitting there as well.

It had been a long time since I'd seen him. Two, three years maybe. His face had filled out, and he was now sporting some stubble. The intervening years had advanced him from a young man into a grown man and the difference was subtle but startling.

'What's going on?'

I thought it was a reasonable question, but nobody tripped over themselves to answer it for me.

Jacob was the one to finally break the silence.

'Mum's been telling me about Martin being released from jail.'

I nodded. It was good that she'd finally broached the subject with him. He had as much right to know in the end as she did, whether or not Terry saw it that way.

'She also mentioned that she's seen him hanging around the crèche at Northland's Mall. She thinks that he's trying to pick out his next victim.'

'Well, she saw him once,' I corrected him, but Terry was shaking her head.

'I saw him again this morning. I followed him for a bit this time. That's why I contacted Jacob. I think that we should make sure that he's not in a position to hurt anyone again.'

'You saw him again?' I waited for her to nod to confirm it. The nod came. 'You saw him and he was hanging about by the crèche?'

The nod came again, but this time there was a crimp in the forehead that told me otherwise.

'Where exactly did you see him?' I pressed.

'He was near the food court again. That's not far away. I'm sure that's what he's up to.'

I sat down at the table next to her. If she'd been a client I would've taken her hand, but knowing Terry she'd just shake off the touch. She wasn't into physical consolation. These days I could sympathise.

'Have you called the police?'

'What good's that going to do? They'll just say that he's not doing anything wrong and they won't do anything until it's too late again.'

'Terry...'

'Oh, don't take that tone of voice with me. What would you know? You think the police do a good job just because you used to help them out with cases. That's bullshit. If they were doing such a good job he wouldn't be out on the streets right now, would he?'

I opened my mouth to retort, but Jacob got in before I had a chance to.

'That's not down to the police. That's down to the parole board. And they wouldn't let him out if they weren't reasonably sure that he wasn't going to do it again. After all, the spotlight will go straight back on them if they're wrong.'

'The spotlight? Like that's some kind of deterrent. We don't even know who makes those decisions. They're not going to give a shit if it goes wrong. The only people who are going to give a shit are the ones whose daughter is being eyed up as an easy target right now.'

'Terry. You may not have much faith in the police, but surely it can't hurt to report his actions to them. If he really is stepping out of line then they'll be the ones to follow up.' I'd almost forgotten that Kendra was there until she spoke. Her voice was full of calm. And Terry could hardly accuse her of putting all her faith in the police.

'I don't know why you're all ganging up on me. I have a right to be concerned.'

'Of course you do Mum. It's just that we don't want you to get out of hand and land yourself in trouble.'

'You just don't want me to get your friend in trouble,' she spat back.

'Terry!' both Kendra and I chorused. Horrified.

Jacob just shrugged it off.

'How are you going to be able to keep an eye on Martin if you're issued with a restraining order or even worse because you won't leave him alone? You need to protect yourself so you can make sure that there's nothing he can do.'

'If you don't want to contact the police, maybe we can let the Mall know that he's hanging around,' mused Kendra. 'If we let them know about our concerns, they can review their CCTV to see if he really is hanging around places that would be of concern, and even if he's not now they might be able to have security track his movements when he's inside the Mall. I'm sure they'll be just as interested in making sure their patrons are safe as we are.'

Terry stuck out her chin in defiance, but mustn't have been able to find anything wrong with the plan because after a minute she acceded to it. 'Alright. I'll give them a call and let them know they've got a resident paedophile.'

'Do you want me to let the police in my station know as well? I could just have a casual chat to see if they've got him on the radar or not?'

Terry nodded again. 'Whatever.'

***

Rena phoned me midway through the afternoon, and I went around to see her.

She seemed to have shrunk since yesterday. Maybe that was just the different surroundings though. I hadn't seen her house before, and I surprised at the age of the property. It was spotless, but it must have been harder when everything was starting to reach the age that it would need to be repaired or replaced to get anywhere within shouting distance of being truly clean and tidy.

'So you know they've let him go?' She said in greeting.

To be honest I didn't know anything after I was dismissed from the scene. I was also surprised. Surely they would need to hold and question Ash for a while to establish what was going on. Still, what did I know?

'I hadn't heard. Has he gone back home.'

She shook her head. 'No - they're still setting that aside as a potential crime scene, whatever that means. If they think he's done it then why isn't he still in custody, and if they don't what do they think happened in his home that they can't let him in it?'

'I suppose sometimes the actions the police take look odd from the outside. I'm sure they wouldn't be doing these things without good reason though.'

'The only good reason I can see is to get Chloe back, and they don't seem to be doing much about that.'

She sighed heavily and sat down. When she resumed speaking her voice was much quieter. Much softer.

'I really thought that it was going to be over. When he didn't come home. I dillied and dallied over telling anyone - well you know that - but when I finally revealed that Ash had run off I really thought that it would just be a matter of time before they brought Chloe back to me.'

A large tear slipped down the side of her face, and she swiped it away angrily with the back of her hand.

'I shouldn't be the one sitting at home crying. That should be my bloody ex-husband. I know he's got more to do with this than he pretended. It's not a coincidence that he fled and then came back beaten to a pulp.'

Another tear, and another. Rena squeezed her eyes tightly shut as though willing them to stop, and when she opened them again it appeared she was successful.

'I did everything right. I didn't talk badly about him in public. I defended him when that awful journalist was making her accusations. I did everything right, in the right order. That means I'm meant to get my daughter back safe and sound. But she's not here is she?'

'Rena this must be a very difficult time for you. If you like, and I really would recommend this, I can organise a counsellor for you to see to talk through all of what you're going through.'

Rena stared at me in surprise. 'But isn't that what you're here for?'

I looked back at her evenly. 'I can listen to you and help out where I can, yes. But I think you may benefit from talking to someone who is professionally trained to help you deal with your emotions, and thoughts. I'm a support volunteer, but I think you could benefit from a professional psychologist to talk to.'

She jumped up and paced the length of the room.

'I really don't get it. When Erik said I should think about contacting you he definitely said that you'd be able to help me out with talking and stuff. He said you were trained.'

And I could add another item to my shit list. Yes, I was a trained psychiatrist, but that wasn't a help in a case like this. Victims needed counselling, not prescription medication. Erik should know bloody better than to be telling my potential clients that. Especially knowing that he couldn't guarantee I'd even be the one to be in touch with them.

The truth was always a good defence. I took the punt and tried it out.

'I am a trained psychiatrist, but that just means I can work with mentally ill people. I'm not trained as a counsellor so I'm not really the person to talk through your experiences with you. If you want a prescription for some anti-depressants I can help you out, but otherwise...' I shrugged.

Rena blushed. 'But I am mentally ill. I mean...' she trailed off, confused. 'Aren't I?'

'Yes but that's not what I'm here to deal with. If you want help with your OCD then that's one thing - although since I don't practice anymore I still wouldn't be of much use - but since I think you could benefit from talking to someone about how you're feeling about Chloe missing, that would require someone else.'

'No,' Rena said slowly, as though considering her options. 'No, I think I'd rather just stay with you for now. I already feel comfortable with you, and I think I'd just be more nervous if I had to deal with another stranger at this point.'

Okay. Not option A or option B but made-up or misunderstood interpretation option C. Great. I thought of the energy necessary to go through the whole ridiculous explanation again, and really couldn't be bothered. And if Rena was comfortable with me, that was good enough. I'd started to feel comfortable with her too, tell the honest truth.

I gave in.

'Okay, but remember the offer's there if you need it.'

Rena nodded emphatically as though in agreement. 'No, I think this is the right choice for me.'

***

I spent much of the day with Rena, waiting for news, helping her out with meal arrangements, talking idly about nonsensical things just to pass the time. All we were really doing was waiting, however. Waiting for someone to find Chloe and bring her home.

The strain of it was pulling me down, but Rena seemed to be coping remarkably well. Of course I hadn't known her before; maybe she was superwoman in her normal life and this was a seriously downgraded version.

When I texted Gary during the day he replied that he was staying at a friend's house for a few nights. He wanted to think things over.

I walked into the empty house and missed him straight away. It was always so much nicer to deal with the Gary in my head and memory than the physical reality. Maybe to keep our marriage working we should live completely separate lives and that way we'd function beautifully. Of course, most people would think of that as a divorce.

I sat down to watch the news before thinking about making something for tea, and then woke hours later in the dead of the night. It seemed a waste to drag myself all the way upstairs just for a few more hours, so I turned over on the couch and went back to sleep.

Having missed eating the night before I felt I really should put something in my stomach for breakfast, but the thought of food left me oddly cold, and I settled for a large cup of coffee. The lethargy of my daily life was dragging on me already. Pulling on my bones until I felt fatigued just standing.

I tried to catch hold of Erik at work, but he seemed to be avoiding me. I didn't really know what I was going to say to him anyway. There's a friend of mine, thinks she keeps seeing a paedophile at the local mall and I'm pretty sure she's making it up but would you be able to keep an eye on him anyhow. Of course I could also berate him over the information he'd passed on to Rena, but then it was hypocritical to expect him to treat me like any other of the volunteers that came through this station, when I kept assuring everyone I was qualified for far better things.

Stevie rolled into the office, and then rolled out again. There were waves of people out in the station. Everything rushed at one moment, and then slow and silent the next.

This wasn't really the life for me anymore. I'd thought it was a good idea when Gary and I came back to New Zealand, but whatever attraction there'd been seemed to exist solely in my imagination. I didn't think I was helping any one in particular, and I certainly didn't feel motivated to put any more of myself into it.

If Rena was the last case I dealt with, would that be too bad?

My phone interjected itself into my reverie. I saw an unknown number and shivered, but forced myself to answer.

'It's Jacob. Can you please meet me down Langdon's Road? I think Mum's gone completely crazy.'

I drove there in a hurry. The damage out North was fairly minimal and the roads were clear with all routes open and operating.

'Jacob,' I yelled out of the car window when I saw him standing at the side of the road.

He ran towards me, and his pace told me that nothing had been resolved in the meantime.

'She's round the back. I told her not to. I told her it's trespassing, but she just won't listen.'

'Round the back of where? Where are we?'

'She says she saw him walking along the street this time. It's in the middle of three school zones, so she followed him. She knocked on the front door for ages, but he wouldn't answer.'

For Christ's sake.

'Terry,' I called out as I followed the path of broken branches and trampled flowers around the side of what was obviously once a State House.

'Terry!'

She was standing with her face pressed against a window. One hand was balancing her by clutching on to a very unstable looking downpipe, the other was pressed flat against the glass and her high heeled toes were sinking into the dirt of a flowerbed as she stretched to her fullest height.

As I came level with her I realised there were net curtains drawn across the windows on the inside. She was trying to squint with her face and eyes on an angle to get a clearer view. I couldn't see any shadows that would indicate an occupant in the room at all.

I caught her arm and pulled her back. I stumbled as her full weight fell against me for a minute, then caught my balance and held her steady while I led her onto the lawn.

'I thought you were going to report him to mall security,' I hissed at her. My voice as low as it would go while I was this angry. 'What happened to the plan?'

'I didn't fucking agree to that. You, Kendra and Jacob did. I don't care what you do - I'm going to make sure that he's not hurting another girl in there while you all stand idly back saying "oh no the parole board wouldn't make a mistake" like it's the first time that ever happened.'

'Fine. But it's not okay to go stalking men around the neighbourhood and then following them home and trying to break in.'

'I'm not trying to break in. I'm trying to look in. I'm going to try to break in later.'

She headed back towards the window, but luckily Jacob joined me around the side of the house and helped me to hold her back.

'Did you see anyone go in there?' I whispered to him.

He shook his head. 'I was just on my way to the dairy when I saw Mum running across the road and starting to pound on the front door. I didn't see anyone.'

'I am fucking here you know,' Terry retorted angrily. 'I can fucking hear every fucking word you're fucking saying about me.'

'Then you fucking know that your fucking son didn't fucking see anyone,' I shouted back. What was the use of whispering if Terry was shouting and pounding? Obviously there was no one home to hear out racket or they'd be out here with us investigating already.

'He didn't see Martin because I waited until he'd gone inside the house before I crossed the street,' she shouted as though that was the most perfect explanation ever. 'It wasn't going to be any use making sure he didn't see me following him if I then ran up as soon as he started to cross the road.'

So obvious. I hadn't passed my stalking 101 recently enough to remember all this stuff.

'If he's in there then why isn't he answering the door?'

Terry stared at me as if I was mental. I was beginning to think that perhaps she was right.

'He's not letting me in because he's got another girl in there that he's molesting, isn't he. Duh!'

She shook off Jacob's hold and went back to the window to try once again to peer in.

'Why do you think he's got a little girl in there?' I tried to reason. 'Was she out walking the streets with him as well?'

'There's no need to be sarcastic. I asked the shopkeeper what he'd bought. He said he bought a six-pack of beer, a Lotto ticket, and four packets of boiled sweets.'

'Jesus Terry. So no man's allowed to buy sweets at the dairy unless they're a child molester?'

'No one eats boiled sweets unless they're too young to afford real sweets or too young to know the difference. When's the last time you thought to yourself "oh yes I could really do with a boiled sweet"? Unless you're under the age of five the answer's never.'

I hated to admit the warped logic was never-the-less logic of a kind. So I wouldn't.

'You can't harass someone on that basis Terry. Come with me now before you really get yourself in trouble. We can talk it through.'

'I'm not one of your patients, and I'm not talking anything through with you. I'm standing here until...'

She broke off as the sound of cars arriving and people running came from the front of the house.

'What?' Jacob said as he headed back around towards the front.

Terry and I stood and stared at each other for a long moment, then we both took off running back to the front. Straight into the path of a uniformed officer heading towards the back.

He stuck his face directly into Terry's and said quietly, 'Don't say a word and get around to the front. Now.'

I was too surprised and frightened to inform him that if he'd wanted a quiet entrance and the element of surprise Terry may have messed that up just a tad. I followed her around, and ran straight out into the stony face of DSS Smith.

'I don't know what you're doing here,' he said with venom. 'And I don't really care at this point. But get into your car and stay there until I come to see you. Is that understood?'

I nodded and headed toward the car, but Terry must have taken issue because I heard Erik, 'That applies to all three of you,' before she and Jacob joined me.

We sat in tense silence. I was mortified that I appeared to have stuffed up some kind of covert operation. I was further mortified that Erik and his team's presence here probably meant that Terry had been perfectly correct in her assessment and that I'd been wrong. How dare that be the case?

'Do you think they're going to arrest us?' Jacob asked after a minute or two had passed.

I watched as a signal passed through the carefully arranged team, and then tensed as Erik approached the front door with a megaphone.

'I doubt it, Jacob. But I'm sure we're all in for a bit of a lecture. I think the most we could get is a caution for trespass and I for one don't plan to make a habit of it.'

'This is the police. Your property is surrounded. Please evacuate the premises slowly, with your hands up.'

One of the officers behind Erik prepped his taser, and stood tensely as they waited for a response they didn't expect to hear.

There was another flurry of signals and nods, and then an enormous ramming device was carried in by two men.

'I repeat, this is the Police. We have reason to believe that you're holding a child against her will. If you don't come out now, with your hands up, we will make entrance.'

I held my breath as my heart beat off the seconds, and then there was a flurry of action. The device was swung back and then forth against the door. It splintered with ridiculous ease, and the men with the device backed away as another two officers, one of them Erik, entered the property. Another two followed soon after with yet another pair standing at the front corners of the house. I imagined the man who'd met us at the side would have a partner around the back with him too.

A muffled cry of 'Here!' emerged from inside, and I felt my muscles tense even further as I strained to listen for more.

Was this Chloe. While I was outside lecturing Terry on her behaviour was the monster who'd murdered her beautiful daughter been inside inflicting his tortures on Chloe? How would I ever be able to live with this?

There was silence. More silence. Then another flurry of activity but this time outwards.

'Christine!' Erik called as his reddened face appeared at the splintered doorway. 'Get your arse in here, now!'

I jumped out of the car and ran towards the entrance, my heart trying to keep a beat going and my head already starting a beration I expected would keep going for a lifetime.

'Stay back,' he called. I tried to stop, then realised he was looking over my shoulder. Good luck with that Erik.

He pushed back past an exiting officer and I followed blindly.

What had he done? What had he done?

Was she still alive? Was that why he was calling me?

I could feel Terry's breath at my shoulder. I wanted to turn and tell her to leave - she didn't want to see this - but my earlier admonitions trapped the words in my throat.

'Here. Quickly,' called Erik from another doorway. There was tiling. Plasterboard. Shower curtain. A bathroom. There was blood. There was blood. There was blood.

Erik pulled aside the curtain to reveal a man in his twenties. Naked in the bath. I tried to see around him, to see where the little girl was, to see Chloe, but there was no one else. My eyes drew back to him and focused.

'Can you help him? I've called the ambulance but he's losing blood and no one's trained for this situation.

What situation? Where was the blood coming from?

I knelt next to the bathtub. Put my hand on Martin's forehead. Then his shoulder. I pushed so that he fell onto his back in the tub. His legs splayed wide. So much blood. A razor blade covered with it. So much blood.

And the penis freshly cut from his body lay limp in the bottom of the tub. Pushing against the drain with the flow of the blood.

CHAPTER SEVEN

Tina's Story

It was the hardest thing I'd ever had to do. To leave my child in a strange country while I went back home. But it was also the best thing I ever did.

I grew up in a warm sunny place, where there was always room to run and play, and there was never enough to eat and drink. I remember when my mother bought me a new pair of sandals when I was eight. They were bright pink and someone had donated them to the charity shop with the tags from the shop still attached. They were the only new thing I'd ever been given; and they were the last new thing I saw for many years.

I wore those sandals until the pink leather ties finally split from the soles. I repaired them with old shoelaces and string and then with tight ribbing from an old lifejacket that had washed up on the beach. I put them back together with glue and needle and thread. I wore them and fixed them and wore them and fixed them until they were brown and grey and as ugly and colourless as everything else I owned.

That's how I remember life in my home country.

Brown and grey. Never having enough to eat; never being comfortable enough to stop worrying about where I would live, where I would stay the night, where I would work to earn my next meal. Struggle and hardship day in and day out until the very thought of going on another day just makes you tired and sore.

When I met David I thought that all my dreams were coming true. I thought that everything I'd heard or read about the lives that other people lived was finally going to come true for me to. He swept me off my feet and into his bed, and then he called the next morning when I doubted he ever would. He talked about taking me out of this place and off to somewhere wonderful. Another land, another country, another continent, another opportunity.

I was scared when I realised that I was pregnant. I was scared to tell him; I was scared David would blanch at the words and his face would go cold and he would tell me that I'll see you around and he wouldn't. I kept the information to myself until I thought that he would notice and ask me himself and then I came clean.

He was happy and excited and I thought he was going to hurt the baby he hugged me so hard. We made plans for the future together, and we flew overseas, and we landed in Auckland and we found a place to live and it was all happy and exciting and wonderful.

We moved, and then moved again. I didn't have the right papers to come into the country, and neither did he. I didn't know what I needed to do to get the right ones, but David kept saying don't worry at least our little one will be born here, at least our baby will be a resident and then we'll both be okay. I believed him and smiled and thought happy thoughts about our future.

I gave birth in hospital and they found out about our status, but we were gone before they could do anything. I gave birth to our baby girl and then we took off. We wanted her to be safe and well and have everything that she was entitled to, and she wouldn't have that if they caught us and made us leave.

We settled in Christchurch after a while. We stuck out like sore thumbs, unlike Auckland, but for some *reason that just meant that everyone left us alone rather than asking us questions. There was work fruit picking, and David could be paid under the table as a brickie, and we got by. I brought my baby girl new clothes to make sure she had the best of everything, and I kept them spotless and fresh and clean and bright pink.*

We worked and we got by and we built a life for ourselves the way that David always said we would. Our baby girl grew into a toddler and then into a child and then we started having arguments about how we would have her go to school without us being found out.

We were still arguing about that one morning when David went off to work. He went off to work in the old Holden Torana that he'd picked up for not very much money. It was beat up and old and it broke down occasionally but David was clever with his hands and always managed to get it going again. The breaks had been sticking occasionally but that was nothing he couldn't handle. Until they stuck and he was in the middle of a roundabout and there was a campervan with tourists who were confidently expecting that everyone would give them right of way, and there was an accident and David didn't come home.

Everything unravelled after that. I identified David's body but there was no paperwork for him and no paperwork for me and no way that I could negotiate out of this one because David never gave me any information on what we should do if it came down to it and now he was dead and any ideas he'd had dead with him.

They didn't know about my girl though. I worried for hours and then called someone who called someone who put me in touch with someone who I handed my girl and her belongings, all her clean new pink belongings, to and then I left the country. I was deported and it was hard and it was full of sorrow but I was also full of joy because my daughter was going to have it all. She was going to have the life that I'd only been able to dream of.

CHAPTER EIGHT

There was hauling in and out of offices. There was explaining of fragile psyches and how Terry was only trying to protect the greater good of Christchurch. There was stern warnings and promises to keep closer eyes and honest pleas to do better.

And then there was nothing.

Rena called through a couple of times a week. From her point of view the case was not progressing, and I sympathised but could do little else.

Ash was questioned, let go, questioned, let go. Rena let him back into her life once it became obvious that he now knew less about what had happened to Chloe than she did.

He revealed to her, and her to me, that he'd arranged for Chloe to be "picked up" by someone. Someone whom he could describe, but possessed no real details of. Someone who appeared to exist only in bars and meeting points, but had no connection to real life.

Ash had paid good money for the transaction. It was nice to see that even when he was foolishly entrusting the life and well-being of his only daughter to a total stranger he was willing to pay good money for it. Not that the money led anywhere. An account that didn't belong to the person that it was meant to. Once this case was finished and Ash was prosecuted for his part in the failed endeavour there was a large refund coming. But there was no sign of this case closing. I could tell from Erik's posture as he strode in and out, in and out, that there was no news, no follow-ups and no leads.

The less that happened, the less use I was to Rena; the more she let Ash – the keys to her destruction – back into her life, the less use I was to Rena.

I started meeting with new victims, helping and supporting newly traumatised members of the public. The Sutherland's were not taking up any of my time, any longer.

Terry pouted and sulked and shot warning beams in my direction for a week or more, and then all at once relented. Jacob was mysteriously cast back into outer darkness; his attempts to stop her hurting herself or someone else were a betrayal. I knew better than to argue with a crazy person. It would be like arguing with myself.

Our group met each Monday, and we kept talking around the subject we met for. Our children were gone, and like Rena's child they showed no sign of coming back.

***

Gary was out for most of the afternoon, so I took the opportunity to cook a standing rib roast with an accompaniment of freshly roasted new potatoes – it was the first of the new season Jersey Bennies and my mouth was watering before I even put them into the shopping basket – and a side of salad that I'd probably throw out after stabbing it ineffectively with a fork a couple of times.

I heard him pull up in the car. I really should do something about it; I'd attended enough RTAs when I was on the force to never want to let another drunk drive on the streets, but it was yet another thing I couldn't find the energy to fight at the moment. With any luck he'd be pulled over in a random breath test; that was my best hope. I shoved to the side the thought that the other end was both bloody and likely me to lead to me hating myself for the rest of my life.

Gary made it to the door, and then there was nothing more than scratching noises. I waited and started to time it on the kitchen clock. When it got to 10 minutes I'd had enough and went to open the door for him. The door that he'd been failing to unlock with his key, and didn't seem to realise had been unlocked the whole time.

'Hey honey.' He walked straight past me and then belatedly tried to turn and land a kiss on my cheek. I needn't have worried about flinching away, he fell to one side and after scrabbling at the wall for a moment landed on the floor.

'Oops,' he announced with good humour. 'Lost my footing there.'

'You certainly did,' I retorted as I leant down to give him a hand up. I put my arm around his side and helped him through to the couch. He must have thrown up at some point during the day; he hadn't quite managed to miss his shirt during the process. I tried to unbutton his top, but he kept playfully slapping my hands away, and he then grabbed me and started to tickle me. I've never stood up to tickling well.

'Stop, stop,' I gasped at last, when I started to truly think I wouldn't be able to breathe. 'Take off your shirt yourself then, mister. It needs a wash.'

'Aye, aye Cap'n.'

It was hard to watch my husband, once beloved now tolerated, try to work the tiny buttons with his big drunk hands.

'Let me,' I said, just as he got fed up and pulled it with force.

It cured two of the buttons certainly; they popped off with one landing on the smoked glass coffee table and the other rolling under the loveseat opposite.

I could've fixed the buttons, but there wasn't much chance of pulling together the giant rip where the cloth had given way next to the doubled up buttonhole seam. I could fix a button, repair a tear, but I wasn't a bloody dressmaker.

'Just throw it out then,' I said and waved vaguely in

the direction of the kitchen and the rubbish bin, in case Gary had forgotten.

He used various items of furniture to steady himself as he progressed across the room. God knows how he'd managed to drive himself home from wherever he'd been holed up all afternoon.

'Roast. You cooked me a roast. How did you know I would be so hungry?'

I followed him through into the kitchen and quickly removed the carving knife and fork from his hand. With my luck he'd trip and fall straight onto the knife and then I'd be done for murder. If I'm going down for something I at least want to have the satisfaction of doing it.

'Sit down at the table then. How many potatoes?'

A routine question. It was always enough to fill up the plate, except for the meat. I started to serve, and then turned to look at Gary as he hadn't given me the rote answer.

He'd fallen unconscious at the table.

His head was laid neatly between the cutlery, like he'd served up himself. I moved the knife and fork to one side and then pushed him back gently in his chair. His head rolled to one side and his eyelids flickered briefly but he didn't wake up. The change in position did cause a reverberating snore to replace his usual muffled breathing.

I went back to the bench and pushed half the potatoes off the plate and pushed them back into the baking paper package they'd been cooked in. I served up a full size steak from the rib roast and took it back to the table.

I didn't eat as much as I thought I would. My appetite faded with every snore from my husband. His hair had faded to complete grey over the last couple of years. I hadn't really noticed before consciously – I hadn't really looked at him full-on for a while. Deep lines cut into the side of his mouth, and in contrast to his hair burst capillaries had painted his face a deep red.

His skin, a beautiful tan when I first met him, had faded. The effect was weird; it was as though he was fading away. Like a Cheshire cat; except instead of a smile there'd soon be nothing left of him but a splatter of burst veins.

I wanted to shake Gary awake and take him upstairs, but I couldn't. Tamsin sat between us, an unwelcome guest. The light of my life had turned into a burden. My husband was dying from drink, I was dying from solitude; the only life in the house was the one I lived precariously through other people.

I should've taken action well before this. I knew the signs of alcoholism like the back of my hand. Gary deserved to have a wife who would support him, without enabling him. Drive him to recovery, kicking and screaming if need be. I knew all the old maxims – you can't help an alcoholic unless he wants help; an alcoholic won't stop until he's hit rock bottom – weren't true. If you could get someone into recovery, even against their will, the chances were they could reclaim their life. Even if the effect was only temporary, it was still worth it to live a portion of your life free of drink that to never even have that.

And I could've helped him out of it. I still could. I still should.

I tipped the majority of my tea into the rubbish bin and headed upstairs. It was only just past seven, but I needed to lie down. I was so tired. I needed to lie down, and if I started crying until I finally fell into a half-sleep then that was what I'd do.

***

Wednesday 13th November
Breaking News: Sutherland's tried to kidnap own daughter
While his wife broke down in front of press cameras every day, begging for her daughter's safe return, the man who had arranged and paid for Chloe's abduction stood next to her on the front doorstep, his arm around her shoulder's to support her, never letting on that he knew the truth of what had happened to their daughter.

The article wasn't the worst hatchet job I'd ever read. It didn't need to be. What Ash had arranged for his own daughter may have been motivated out of caring for her; more likely it was about wanting to control her and through Chloe his ex-wife, but still he hadn't set out to hurt anyone except Rena as a side-effect. But, if the McCanns could be vilified for leaving their children alone in a hotel room 50 metres from where they were eating; if the Chamberlains could be hunted and locked up for leaving their baby daughter asleep in a tent in a communal camping ground; hiring someone to kidnap your own child had to carry some serious tabloid recriminations.

The article wasn't bad – the comments were.

For every *stay strong, kia kaha* and *our thoughts are with you I know she will come home to you safe* there was a *peeple dont deserve kids they shud be shot* and a *corse she new too theyve properly sold her there scum and a youll go straight to hell for wot you did you demons.* Whoever opened up online articles for comments to the general internet public – i.e. the public who don't worry about what others thought of them because no one knew who they were – deserved to be shot. Or moderated out of existence. A job the online moderator appeared to have abandoned wholeheartedly in the pursuit of the perfect piece of venom.

After reading it in the morning, and then checking in periodically to make sure it really was as bad as I thought it was, there was no surprise that Rena called through to me. The only surprise was that she took so long. A bit insulting even. Still, I was going to be there for her in a way she hadn't required in few weeks. I actually seemed to have missed her.

'Hi Rena, are you calling about the magazine?'

There was a pause, and I wondered if I'd overstepped the mark somehow. I felt a second of pure fear as the idea insinuated itself in my head that she was unaware of the article and I'd just alerted her to its presence.

But that wasn't it.

'Yes, and no. It was a stupid idea to do that. I knew it, and I think Ash knew it too, but we were just so sick of having nothing done. Even if the piece came out a bit sharp,'

Rena was far more understated than I'd given her credit for...

'... it still achieved putting Chloe back into the public view.' She signed deeply. 'It sounds stupid, but I'd rather people were talking about us and Chloe in a bad light, than not thinking of us at all.'

'It doesn't sound stupid at all,' I reassured her. 'It sounds like you're desperate for some progress, and you have every right to be. Have the police made any comment on it?'

'Not that I've heard. They could've told Ash, he's been in again this morning, but if so he hasn't passed it on. Look, I was really calling about something else.'

'Okay?'

There was a minute or more of silence, but I let it stretch out without breaking. I'd grown used to Rena's rhythm and knew that it took her a while to phrase things in her head before she could speak. Interrupting her just put her thought process back to square one and ended in more silence.

'There's a woman who's been in contact.'

She paused again, but my stomach clenched as I realised what was coming. Vultures love to flock to the scene of a fresh kill. I'd experienced them, Kendra had been pestered for years – off and on – and even Terry with the certain knowledge of her daughter's last days had encountered one or two.

'She says she's a psychic.'

'Rena, I...'

'I know what you're going to say. It's nothing I haven't thought myself already. I know that it's all going to end in nothing. I know that. But if I ignore her I'm scared that I'll be living with a voice in my head saying "you didn't do everything you could." Even if this all blows up in my face, I don't want to have that in my head.'

'Rena, I know these people. I've dealt with them myself, and I've dealt with the fallout from the encounters they've had with my friends, and I think it's a mistake to let them in.'

There was another pause. Rena's next words caught

me by surprise. 'Is that what you call us? Your clients?'

'What?'

'Do you call us your friends?'

I was about to explain that no, that wasn't what I called the people who I met through victim support. They were definitely my clients. But I didn't. My support group had started out as a group of total strangers I pulled together for support, and we ended up as friends. My only friends.

'Only if I think of you that way.'

'Oh.' There was another silence.

'Would you be able to come around to my house? The woman I was telling you about – she's coming over soon. I'd really like you to be there. I'm afraid of meeting her to be honest.'

I could have told her again not to. But it wouldn't get us anywhere. Better I go over and pick up the pieces than abandon Rena just because she made a decision I didn't agree with.

'I'll be there. Give me half an hour.'

***

Rena greeted me at the door, and let me in. There was a media throng gathering outside once again. Rena rubbed her hands together as though spreading on hand cream, and looked nervously over her shoulder.

'Are you okay? Is she here?'

'No. No, she's still on her way. She wants me to show her Chloe's room and sit with her there. I don't like that.'

'Then don't do it,' I said, touching her once on her upper arm. 'If she is genuine then she shouldn't need to be located in a specific room, should she?'

'Really?' Rena looked thoughtful, her face creased into a frown. 'I don't know. It seemed reasonable at the time, but now I don't like the idea.'

'Then just have her sit in the lounge. It's more important that you feel comfortable, than she does. At least that's what I think.'

'What were they like?'

'Hmmm?' I answered vaguely. I hadn't been in

Chloe's room, although I knew where it was. Every time I'd been in this house it had been like a reverse magnet. You could feel it, but everything repelled away from the vicinity.

Rena blushed. 'You said that you'd dealt with psychics before. What were they like?'

I shrugged. 'They were nice to talk to. Lots of closing their eyes and trying to feel the spirit kind of thing. Think of any television psychic you've ever seen, on any TV show, and you'll be thinking along the right lines.'

'You mean like "Sensing Murder"?'

'God no. I don't watch that shit.' I stopped short as I realised how harsh that sounded. 'I meant any, um, scripted television show you might see. I don't know about the unscripted ones.'

'Oh. Right.' She leaned forward and whispered. 'I don't watch much TV. Do you think that's okay?'

I nodded. 'I'm sure it won't make any difference.'

'I know that I said I wasn't expecting anything out of this, but...'

Rena didn't need to finish that sentence. The need and hope was written all over her face. I put the slow burn of anger aside for the time being. The hope and need was what they feed on, trying to pretend it was only ever for someone else's sake but always, always, for their own.

I wished I could say to Rena not to hope, not to want, not to give them the satisfaction. But there was no way of shutting that tap off once it'd started. I hoped this experience wouldn't run her dry.

'Where's Ash?'

'I don't know. I kicked him out.'

I stopped my pacing and stared hard at Rena. That was new. The last time I'd seen her she'd been desperately trying to forgive him for what he'd done – to her and to Chloe – and not quite making it.

'Is he back at his house?'

Rena snorted with something that sounded suspiciously like satisfaction. 'I believe the police have still got that cordoned off as a crime scene. I believe that he may be having to fend for himself right at the minute.'

I can't imagine that would be easy for him in the current Christchurch rental housing market. Even finding hotels or motels empty for anything more than the occasional gap between EQC occupants was hard. That's why Gary didn't need to stay sober.

'You didn't want him to be part of this.'

Rena leaned her head to one side. 'I'm beginning to think that he doesn't deserve to be part of anything anymore. Certainly not this.'

She sat down on the edge of the couch. From there she could keep her eyes on the side window for people approaching the door. Given the journalists outside I was sure we'd have other indicators as soon as anyone arrived.

I was right about that.

Before we could even hear the sound of a car approaching we saw the wave of movement from the media outside. Then a car door slammed shut. Then shouted queries and another wave of movement, and then Rena was pulling open the door, and a woman was rushing inside with the door slammed shut on a cloud of boom mikes.

'Rena?'

The woman was petite and well-put together. A pale blue chiffon blouse over a lace chemise and a fitted black pencil skirt. Her hair was pulled sharply back in a bun. If she'd had glasses she would've looked like a librarian from any high-school movie since the genre began, but her face was bare. Of make-up too.

'My name is Sarah Jones. I called earlier about your daughter?'

'We're aware who you are,' I said. My voice was sharp enough for a frown to appear both on Sarah and Rena's faces.

Sarah turned from me, and looked solely at Rena.

'I feel that this would work better in private. Can I talk to you alone?'

My mouth opened to refuse, but Rena beat me to the punch.

'That would be fine. I know you wanted to see Chloe's room, but I'm not sure I can.'

Sarah stood on tiptoes and put her hands on Rena's shoulders. 'That's fine. We don't have to go there if you're not comfortable with that. Any room is fine.'

It was what I'd said earlier, but it infuriated me to hear it coming out of her mouth.

She looked nothing like the other psychics I'd run into over the years. Most of them had the casual flowy flowery theme going on, as though the seventies had never moved on. I didn't know what to make of her, and her calm voice. I felt rude for my earlier outburst, which made me even angrier with her.

Rena led her out of the room, and I knew better than to follow. I sat in the seat Rena had previously vacated, and watched the media throng outside. The more I stared into the media, the more the media stared into me.

There was a cry of distress from above me, and I ran upstairs feeling energised and vindicated.

I pushed into a room cluttered full with books, and sewing equipment, and the tangled wires of a thousand lost chargers. Rena stood with her hand over her mouth, and tears flowing down her face.

'What? What's happened?' I demanded.

Rena turned to me, and shook her head gently. 'It's not good news.'

'What's not good news?' I looked to Sarah, but she was seated calmly looking at Rena. I turned back to her.

'Sarah has spoken with Chloe. She knows where her body is located.'

I felt the fury turn up a notch to white hot. Yes, Chloe had been missing for weeks now. No, there weren't any leads, there hadn't been any progress and the likelihood right from the start was that there wasn't going to be a happy ending. But for someone to wade in and take away all hope with no more knowledge than a dog in the street wasn't right. It wasn't fair. And I was appalled that Rena just accepted it despite her earlier misgivings.

It could still be right to hold out hope. Chloe hadn't been taken off the street by a complete stranger; okay she had, but there had been planning and execution behind it and a personal relationship formed with a parent. The odd circumstances meant that we had nothing to compare it to, no bar had been set.

When children were taken by people close to them there were two options; one was they were sick fucks who deserved to be locked away forever; two was they wanted a child of their own and felt they had some right to the one they took.

It could be a friendly kidnap in disguise, in which case there would be more hope of a good outcome for Chloe, although that still may not be a reunion with her family. It just meant she would be alive, but perhaps being maltreated in a million different subtle or unsubtle ways every day.

I was surprised and then felt stupid. Sarah was touting herself as a psychic, she was hardly going to tell a story of where Chloe could be located alive.

'How did she die?' I asked in a whisper, hoping that compassion wasn't the wrong response.

Sarah turned her head toward me and smiled. 'I know what you think Mrs Emmett, but you're wrong.'

I just stared at her then turned back to Rena who shrugged.

'I don't know. Sarah hasn't told me yet.'

I turned back to Sarah with my eyebrows raised. I didn't trust myself to speak.

'I don't know all of the details. But as I was just explaining to Mrs Sutherland I can feel a presence that has the aura of her daughter, and that presence has passed.'

I suppressed a shudder at the choice of language. The euphemism of the moment for death creeped me out a hundred times more than just using the accurate description. I was also caught between the sight of some poor soul passing a kidney stone, and someone wandering lost around a blackened other world scene; never being able to come back to what they knew. Give a me a straightforward 'dead' any day.

'Was she murdered?' I asked, then paused in surprise. I didn't mean to interact with the crazy.

Sarah maintained her focus on Rena, and took her hand before saying quietly, 'I'm sorry to say but she was.'

Rena hitched in her breath.

'Was it Ash's fault?' she asked. There was an edge to her voice.

'No.' Sarah paused for a long minute, then resumed; her face harder, her tone harder. 'It wasn't Mr Sutherland's fault. It was the fault only of the man responsible. You are not to blame.'

'Was she in pain?'

Sarah looked reluctant for a moment, then nodded. 'She was in pain. Towards the end. I won't lie to you. It wasn't the worst death that you could imagine, but it also wasn't the easiest.'

'You said a man was responsible for her death,' I interjected. 'Could you give us a description of him? An address?'

There was a pause and then Sarah turned her brilliant violet eyes to mine. She didn't look irritated, she didn't look calm. Her body appeared to hum with some strange sort of energy as she locked her eyes with mine. I shivered, and the moment was past.

'I can describe him, but it won't help you. The police already have his description on file; they have the name he was using on file; they have the details that Chloe could pass on already in their possession. It won't help you.'

'It was the man Ash talked to? The man he paid?'

'It was the man who tricked him,' Sarah replied. 'The man who told him nothing but lies.'

'Where is my baby girl's body?' asked Rena. 'I want to hold her again. Where is she?'

Sarah closed her eyes in concentration. A minute passed; two. Sarah's whole body jerked suddenly and she opened her eyes and turned them to me. Her pupils flicked from side to side; like someone was shaking a liquid die at speed. I felt the hard wall against my back and realised that I'd drawn back from her.

'It wasn't her. It wasn't Tamsin.'

'What?' I was taken aback. I couldn't place the words in order even though they all seemed to be English.

'There was a girl tangled in the power lines. You only saw her for a moment before you were pushed under again. It wasn't Tamsin. It was a local girl; she'd been sent out to collect some fruit from the market. She was worried. Her mother had told her that she had to get the right amount, but she'd only given her a tiny amount of money so she'd have to haggle, and she hated to haggle. It felt like begging; it felt like they couldn't afford to pay the prices they should. And the wave came. She was caught by the power lines, they twisted on either side of her neck and she couldn't breathe. And the water continued to suck her body down until she was underwater again and she couldn't breathe. The wires loosened in the water; they let her body go free. She tried to draw a breath but there was nothing but the mucky water; in her eyes; in her ears; in her mouth; in her lungs. The pain is incredible. So much pain it overrides the need to breathe. It burned. It burns.'

Sarah's body jerked again and she appeared to be gagging or choking, then she collapsed limp in the chair.

I was still pressed hard against the wall. I wanted to be further away.

Rena's voice shook as she queried, 'She drowned? My Chloe drowned?'

I shook my head – no. I continued to shake it, though whether in denial or an attempt to clear it of all the horrible thoughts that had just rushed into it I didn't know.

'No,' I said at last when it appeared that Rena still didn't understand. 'Chloe didn't drown. She's talking about my daughter.'

'Not your daughter,' Sarah interjected. I tried to turn and face her but I couldn't so I continued to look toward Rena. 'It wasn't your daughter. It was another girl. A local girl. Your daughter didn't die.'

'But Chloe? What happened to Chloe?' Rena pressed, looking from me to Sarah and back to me.

Sarah squeezed her hand and let it go.

'I don't know the details of her death. I'm sorry, but sometimes it's like that. I know where her body is though. I can help you with that much.'

As she started to say the answer I wanted to roll my eyes, shake my head. I would, but I was still freaked out enough to need all my energy to just breathe.

'She's either in or near a body of water. There are trees nearby. A lake. Or a pond.'

Sarah reached out and picked up Rena's hands again and squeezed.

'I can take you to her. The spot came to me clearly. I can take you back to your daughter.'

***

I thought it would be easier to explain it to Erik in person rather than try to phone it in as a tip. I tried to call him but I couldn't get through, and Hayley wouldn't ask him to call me back unless I explained what I needed.

And I wasn't going to explain this to her. She was the equivalent of a bloody PA.

Instead I went back to the station myself. I was astonished to see that the sun was high overhead. It felt like I'd been trapped in that room with Sarah and Rena for days, but it was only creeping toward lunch-time.

I couldn't talk normally as I sat at my desk. I couldn't act normally and have a laugh with Stevie. My mind felt like it had shattered into a million bright sparks of light. None of them connecting.

This wasn't the way it was meant to go. I was meant to be sitting with Rena telling her calmly that it hurts when you've got your hope up, but these people bring nothing but disappointment and despair. I should be explaining that they really think they're helping, that they don't understand the harm they're causing. Instead I gripped the edge of my desk in case I went sailing off this flattened Earth.

When I caught sight of Erik I flew through the office to intercept him. I wouldn't let him turn me aside, and I wouldn't let him fob me off. He was not looking happy when he eventually relented and took me into his office and shut the door. He was definitely not looking any happier in the minutes afterwards.

I explained it all calmly to Erik. Then abruptly. Then rudely. Until he grasped that he was going to do this. He was going to follow this mad-woman's instructions. Although, by the end I didn't know if the mad-woman was Sarah or if it was me.

'I didn't pick you as the type,' he said repeatedly until I wanted to smash his smug face in. Long years of dealing with irrational people had given me the strength to hold back however.

'It's not anything to do with believing the crazy bitch,' I finally snapped and shouted. 'But you don't have any new leads, the family want to follow up on this one, the location is extremely precise, and you have a duty to follow up when someone knows the location of a dead body. You're going to do it whether I convince you or not, because you don't have a choice so stop trying to make me beg.'

'Too late. You already said please about three different times.'

My face gave him pause, and his tone abruptly changed.

'You're right of course, Christine. Of course we'll do it. I'm sure it will give Mrs Sutherland great comfort to stand in a muddy field while we dredge a pond with nothing in it for a day or two because she forgot to run off the crazy brigade when they turned up. You'll be there too, won't you?'

That was a stupid question.

'Wouldn't miss it.'

***

There was no one home again when I made it through the door. I shouldn't be surprised after this long. It happened at least half the time. But my mind resolutely held onto a more peaceful time in our relationship where he would let me know where he was going and what he was doing, and I would reciprocate, and we would both know where we stood. It was a time that receded further into the past every day.

I lay on the couch and watched the TV for a while. Rena was on there, twitching curtains as a television camera operator stood outside voicing concerns the article had raised.

It was amazing how in the passage of the last 24 hours Rena and Ash had managed to go from being a small article in the paper about how there was still no progress, to being a headline act with psychic overtones.

When I went upstairs I found that most of the bedding should be aptly renamed flooring and set about remaking it into a reasonable place to sleep. I also fetched my sleeping pill stash from the back of the medicine cabinet hidden inside a shaving head replacement box.

I felt both stupid and stupidly reassured by the act of hiding my medication. Something I would ponder another time, along with the consideration that my daughter hadn't drowned years ago. Sometime in the next decade maybe, if I felt strong enough.

I took a tablet downstairs, and pulled out a box cutter to split it along the midway line, then stopped. After the day I'd had, I might throw a full pill down the hatch and not leave sleep to chance at all. I popped it in my pocket for later retrieval, then looked blankly in the fridge until it began to rudely beep at me. When the hell did I start to get appliances that talked back?

The knock at the door was a welcome reprieve from all the thought that was not going on. But it was not so welcome when I saw the sight on the other side.

Ethan and Gary stood sheepishly on the front step. Gary was obviously drunk; he swayed back and forth like a branch in a breeze, absent the breeze. Ethan just looked embarrassed to be there. Embarrassed and slightly annoyed. Reality hit me.

'He's been caught drunk driving?'

I asked it, but the more I looked at the two of them the more certain I became it was actually a statement of fact.

'He was pulled over when his car was reported by another driver. He had been attempting to drive along the side of the road, right at the side of the road, where everyone parks, and when they gave him the breath test he was over.'

That was a polite way of putting it. By the looks of

him Gary was almost at the point where he was close to overdosing and dying more than just being incapable of driving well.

'Gary, go inside and sit down,' I snapped at him.

He obeyed and I listened with my eyes closed as I heard his progress inside the house. I flinched when I heard the sound of the silver fruit bowl my mother had given me as a twenty second birthday present toppled to the ground. But it would survive this. Even if it now sounded like Gary had put his foot on it as well, it would be right as rain with a bit of home administered panel beating. Not like the vase my mother had given me for my twenty fifth birthday which was now long deceased.

When I opened my eyes again I saw the expression on Ethan's face and I almost flinched again. I saw myself and Gary through his eyes for a second. The couple that used to be the life of the party; intelligent and fun. And then their daughter dies and you don't know what to say to them anymore. Their daughter dies and they're no longer fun to have around. Their daughter dies and they both start to go off the rails.

Ethan had been at Gary and my wedding. He'd seen how much we'd been in love, and how much we'd teased each other with rampant good humour. And now I was a harridan and Gary was a drunk. And the dead daughter was now so far in the past it was hard to keep remembering that we were the couple that had to be treated with kid gloves. Not when any decent couple would've got over it by now. Would've found a new path in life. But not the Emmetts – they were still wallowing in their own self-pity until they were an embarrassment to be around. That's why no one came around anymore.

'Thanks for bringing him home Ethan. What's going to happen to him?'

'Court case in a few months. He's five times legal so his license has already been taken off him. The car should've gone to impound but I've parked it around the back of the station instead. You can pick it up any time.'

'Thanks Ethan.'

He nodded, and then looked behind him longingly at his own vehicle.

'Why don't you head off now?' I suggested to help him back there. 'I need to have a word with Gary and I don't want you to take any longer on this than you already have.'

I expected he would jump at the invitation to leave, but he stood there moving his weight from the ball of one foot to the other.

'He was five times legal Christine.'

'You already said.'

'Five times. He could've killed somebody.'

I just looked at him and wished that he'd go away.

'You know he's been taking the car out in this state, don't you?'

Again I said nothing, just stared.

'Christine, I don't want to tell you how to run your life, but it's not okay to let him do that. He obviously needs to get some help, some serious help. You can't let him use the car in this state again. Do you understand?'

'I understand Ethan. I'll hide the keys.'

He slammed his fist into the side of the doorway, and I jumped with the noise and with shock. Ethan was the calmest person I know.

'That's not what I'm talking about Christine. You need to get him serious help. Hiding the car keys isn't going to do shit, and you of all people know it. You need to get him in a program and get him back to reality or this is all going to end badly.'

He leaned forward, and I flinched back. I think it was that motion that made him stop and reconsider. He took a step back instead.

'Get him some help. And get yourself some while you're at it. Your house looks like a tip compared to all the others,' his hand did a wide sweep of the neighbourhood where ours was the only unkempt front yard. 'It's been long enough. You both need to get back on track.'

'Yes sir,' I snarled back at him, and then slammed the door before he could try to break any more home truths to me.

I started to cry and rested my head against the door. I heard Ethan walking away. I stood there for long minutes until I needed a tissue and went into the kitchen to find one. I could hear Gary's snore; at least I wouldn't have to deal with him for the time being. When I'd blown my nose and for myself back under control I went through to the lounge and looked at the source for all this trouble. It would be so easy, I thought. It would be so easy to just pick up a cushion and have this whole thing over in a few minutes. Gary wouldn't even wake up in his state. He'd never even know about the struggle for breath. He'd just stop. And when he was done I could take the rest of my stash of sleeping pills and I could just stop too.

***

I was lost in my own thoughts as I drove Rena and Ash out to the location indicated by Sarah Jones. There was a honk at one point as I made a turn without indicating, and I reminded myself to be more careful. I was going to be the sole driver in the household so I couldn't lose my license too.

When I'd picked up Rena and realised Ash was beside her I thought for a minute that they'd reconciled. Her stony face turned deliberately away from his in the backseat reassured me that they definitely had not.

The forecast had been for sunshine with a bit of cloud, but when you live in Christchurch for any length of time you grow used to treating the weather forecast like a poor guess. Grey skies overhead meant that the drizzle had settled in for a good long while. If I'd been a betting woman I'd have said for as long as we were forced to stand next to this pond while the dive team worked to uncover nothing.

Sarah Jones turned up late, and immediately went over to stand with the Sutherlands. Erik talked with the dive team leader, whether discussing strategy or how long they had to spend time like performing monkeys before we could all pack up and head off home I don't know.

The area would be beautiful in sunlight. A long bank of poplar trees acted as a windbreaker around the paddock, and there was a wonderful rock lined creek leading down to the pond. I wondered what it was that defined a pond from a lake. I was fairly certain that if the same body of water had been in the middle of the city park it would have been called a lake and named after a queen.

Apart from the poplars there were also weeping willows dotted about the area. I always loved these trees; they shouted Christchurch at me in a way no other landmark could. Especially now so many of our man-made landmarks were broken.

Erik broke away from the dive team and headed back my way. 'Shouldn't you be over there offering support to the Sutherlands?' he asked as he joined me. 'I presume the lovely lady over there with them is the great psychic of the west? Does she make you uncomfortable Christine?'

'Whatever. I'm not in the mood to be listening to a weirdo telling me tales from my dead mother.'

Erik stared at me, probably wondering what side of the bed I'd got out of. Then he remembered another richvein of amusement for himself.

'A little bird told me your husband was on the wrong side of the law last night. You want to put him on a tighter leash. Can't have the people who work beside me in the station flagrantly disregarding the law. It makes us look bad.'

'As if you need any help,' I muttered under my breath. Erik gave me a look that I anticipated heralded the beginning of a long lecture, so I went over and stood with the Sutherlands.

'...and I'll be here for you,' I heard Sarah finish off as I arrived. She looked at me curiously, then nodded her head and smiled. 'Lovely to see you Ms Emmett. I'm glad you're here in support of Rena and Ash as well. They may need it today.' She gave Rena a shoulder pat, as if that was comfort from a woman who'd convinced her we were about to dredge her only child's body from a dirty pond in the middle of nowhere. Yep – that must be one hell of a powerful shoulder pat.

'If you need to leave at any time,' I offered the

Sutherlands, already knowing that I would receive firm shakes of the head – which I did.

'Remember you don't have to stay out here. The police will be looking out for Chloe with the same care that you would be. If she is out here they'll handle her with respect.'

Rena grasped for my hand and squeezed it tightly. Too tightly. She was close to the edge. 'I need to be here. I need to see and make sure.' She looked up at me with fear and pleading covering her face. 'I know you understand. Sarah told me about your own troubles.'

I felt a jolt of cold sickness through every part of my body, and a whine started in my ears. I shook my head to clear it and snatched my hand back from Rena. I didn't want to be the one who could understand what she was going through.

I was almost on the verge of heading back Erik's way to see if there was any chance something might happen soon, when there was finally some action. There were three members of the dive team, but only two would enter the water. The third was there specifically to look for signs of distress from his two team members, and also to facilitate if they required any equipment in the water.

The two started off in different directions, and swam on the surface of the water. They would have a grid to search, so even if there was anything to find it could take a while.

The drizzle continued steadily. Although the day wasn't too cold, between the grey cloud cover not allowing a single ray of sunshine through, and the constant dampness from the sky, I was soon shivering. I shifted from foot to foot to try to generate some measure of heat, and also as a slight relief to the boredom of watching not much happen.

One of the team dove down under the surface, and I stilled. Had he found something?

I watched as he re-emerged then swam over to the side of the pond where his team mate stood waiting.

There was a bit of pointing, a bit of discussion, and then they called through the walkie-talkie to the third man. He joined them.

My hands tensed into fists, and I looked back to see how Rena and Ash were reacting. Ash's mouth was slightly parted, and otherwise his face was completely still. His eyes didn't break for a blink as he focused on the men on the other side of the pond. Rena also slowly tracked the movement.

The huddle broke apart and the dive team returned to their previous positions. On the right hand side of the pond the dive member resumed his grid search, but the other member went back to the spot he'd been at and dove down again.

Erik signalled to me on the other side of the pond and I walked around to meet him.

'There's a problem,' he said by way of greeting.

'We noticed. What's going on?'

'There's some sort of sinkhole in the centre of the pond. The divers going back in to assess how deep but he said there's a ledge, and then a well straight down. The bottom just drops away.'

The diver still following the grid pattern, signalled to the shoreman, and then also dived.

'Looks like they've found the other side,' Erik said.

We waited until the divers surfaced and came back to the shoreline, and then both headed around.

'It's within regulation depth,' the shoreman said as we approached. I liked a man who got straight to the point. 'We can dive it, but we'll need to set up a different search system. We'd like to send a camera down first, scan the whole area if we can, and then if it finds something that warrants further investigation we send in the boys.'

'How long?' Erik barked, looking distinctly unimpressed that his futile search was creeping up in value every second.

'We've got the equipment here, but it depends on the clarity down at the bottom. Tony here thinks that the visibility is okay but there's some sort of problem with aeration.'

'What does that mean?'

'If the oxygen levels are low there's going to be a lot of

dead pond life down there. There could be a lot of false signals.'

'Whatever,' Erik said grumpily. 'Just get it done.'

They set up again, and just over three quarters of an hour later the camera started its journey back and forth across the bottom of the pool.

I waited with the Sutherlands and Sarah for any developments. I was interested to see how even though Rena and Ash were placing trust in Sarah's predictions, they were still both fervently holding out hope she was wrong.

I knew what that was like. Gary knew it even better.

It may seem cruel but I hoped that they would have some confirmation today. It's hard to see from outside, but sometimes the hope or belief that your child is alive and well but just somewhere you'll never see them again is even harder to bear than the knowledge that they've gone forever. I've seen how that hope and belief wears people in the group down a little more year after year after year, while the grief that people hold when they have surety lessens at the same rate. It doesn't make sense; but it's so.

Sarah stared at the pond along with the Sutherlands. I had to give her a nod, she was certainly earning her money out here today. She talked with a soft, low voice to them occasionally, most of it out of my earshot but with the rhythm of gentle reassurance or condolence. Her only nervousness showed in her repeated grab at the silver ballet dancer that hung on a thin silver chain around her neck. She pulled it back, and forth. Back, and forth.

It was an hour or more before there was a shout that startled us all out of our individual reveries. I took a step toward the dive site, but at the waving gestures and quick movements on the shoreline it became clear that the cord feeding into the camera had become caught.

I paused on the balls of my feet, leaning toward the minor action, hoping for the long wait to be over, but as everyone fell back into their previous places I stepped back into position.

'Rena, would you like me to take you to the car?' I

asked when I caught sight of a grimace of pain. The deepening cold must be eating into her recently healed bones. 'You can have a lie down in the back seat, and I'll keep a look out at what's happening and tell you what's going on. You won't miss anything.'

I thought she'd refuse, but she nodded and we moved off to my vehicle.

'Are you okay? You don't have to be here for this. I'm quite happy to drive you home.'

'And what good would that do? I'll still be waiting to find out what happened. I think I'd rather be here. I know it's silly, but I think that if I put up with this little bit of misery it makes it more likely that Chloe won't be here.'

I looked back toward the dive site as Ash and Sarah returned to their previous positions. The constant drizzle and greyness of the day was taking its toll on me too. I felt like crying; I'd already done that yesterday and it wasn't like me at all. I wondered if perhaps I should be looking for someone to talk to, someone to assess me.

'Ho!'

The two divers on land held up their hands as a signal came across the walkie-talkies. Erik went over for another discussion.

'The dive team have just issued a signal,' I relayed obediently to Rena. Probably just the cord again. DSS Smith is heading over to check it out.'

I saw Erik gesticulating as he fired off a quick message, and then I felt coldness moving up my skeleton from the tips of my toes until ice fingers massaged the top of my head. He'd taken a step back from the monitor and turned toward Ash and Sarah.

He'd been looking at them, or rather glaring at them, all day but this was different. This time his face was set with resolve.

I looked back at the lone diver, who'd just been babysitting the apparatus. He pushed the air-piece into his mouth and dived below the surface.

'What is it? What's happening?'

I purposely kept my gaze out across the water. I didn't need Rena to pick up on my concern until it was validated. 'The diver has just dived down to check on something. Maybe the camera is stuck.'

I heard a rustle as Rena attempted to sit up; I was obviously crap at hiding my feelings. I moved to put a restraining hand on her shoulder, and then decided to let her be. If she needed to see then let her see.

Long minutes dragged by as Erik and the two dive team members on land stared fixedly at the camera relay. Then there was a ripple on the surface of the pond as the diver resurfaced, and swam quickly in to shore.

Erik detached himself from the group and walked around to where Ash and Sarah were standing, and then brought them to the car to include Rena.

'They've located a body,' he said bluntly. 'It's not in a state where we can perform an ID but I'd like you to come and have a look at the clothing, and see if matches what Chloe was last seen in.'

'You've pulled her out?' Rena asked from the car as she struggled to stand.

'No. The body is still on the floor of the pond. The second dive team member will take the camera back out with a different lens, and we'll try to get some closer shots.' He paused and looked Rena and Ash straight in the eye. 'I'm sorry. The body is not in a good state, so if you prefer I can describe the clothing to you and you could tell me whether or not that matches.'

'No,' Rena said immediately. 'I want to see. If that's my little girl in there I want to see.'

She reached for Sarah's hand as she walked around to where the equipment was located. Ash held her other hand and shoulder, and I walked behind them feeling like an intruder.

I didn't want to believe the search had located Chloe. It seemed like a wild goose chase from the start. How could they have found the goose? I looked at Erik, and under his grim expression I could see a matching struggle to understand.

Rena had tears slowly dripping down her face that she wiped angrily with the back of her hand in order to have a clearer view. I looked over her shoulder, and as the camera moved position I could make out the muddy pond floor. The only life down there was a thick waving mass of weed. Dark green and grey.

A shape appeared out of the gloom. There was the frilly puff of a shoulder from a dress; pink and green stripes came into focus. The camera turned and followed the angle of the body to follow the lines of the dress then, when it would've reached the neckline, it reversed its direction.

Rena started to shake her head and choked out a laugh. 'It's not her. She doesn't have anything like that in her wardrobe.' She turned to Ash for confirmation and he shook his head - no. 'It's not Chloe.'

She grasped for Ash's hand behind her, and squeezed it until his fingers turned white. 'Ash, it's not her. It's not our little girl.'

Erik placed a hand on Rena's shoulder. 'There's still a chance it could be,' he warned. 'The clothing could have originated from another source.'

'Do you understand that Rena?' I asked quietly. 'You may need to wait until they have further tests done to confirm that it's not Chloe.'

Rena nodded her understanding, but her face told me that she'd written off the idea. It was like a sunshower; tears continued to flow while her mouth continued to beam a smile.

'What's that?' Ash asked, pointing at the screen. The camera had been directed away from the body again, but there was something there.

There was a flash of blue, which receded, then came fully into the screen shot again. The diver's hand appeared in shot as he reached out toward the colour. It reached out and gently pinched blue material between finger and thumb. The material pulled forward, swaying in the water flow, and then a white shape filled the screen and rolled over to one side. Eye sockets and a white grin.

Rena screamed as the skull filled the screen.

CHAPTER NINE

Kendra's Story

I was such a good girl when I was little. I was shy, used to hide in my mother's skirts when she tried to introduce me to people, or sometimes even when people I knew well and liked came by and I just wasn't in a 'friends' mood.

Because I was shy I wouldn't ever break any rules. I was frightened enough by the everyday tasks I had to puzzle and struggle my way through, without adding to the horror with additional mayhem. I would sit quietly in class, at home, at church, and look at all the other kids cutting up rough and envy them with a deep pulsing envy. I would fantasize at night about how I would gather my courage and act out – just a little bit, or maybe a lot – I would go through every single detail over and over in my mind until the thoughts were almost as strong as a memory. And then the next day I would sit quietly unless asked to contribute, and I wouldn't put a foot wrong.

A permanent fear of sleep made me obsessively count down the time from the moment I woke up until the moment the worst part of the day arrived and I was forced to go to bed and spend long hours staring at the ceiling and hoping that I wouldn't fall asleep. Lying awake was bad – waking up from a nightmare was a million billion times worse. Feelings of happiness were always checked against the current time, and then reassessed in light of how close it was to bedtime.

Good and scared. Good, and scared. That was me. Day in and day out for year after year after year. Getting good marks in every class because I was bright and because I was good. Paying attention in every class because I was meant to, and doing my homework every night because I was meant to. And on, and on, and on it went.

Until I turned into a teenager. A proper teenager. I didn't like the inside of my head anymore, if I ever had, it was an awful place to visit and to live there was excruciating. So I started trying to get out of it. It was hard as a good girl. There was a lot of sneaking and experimenting and stealing in order to get my hands on anything I could to tune in, turn on and drop out. My parents may have watched their alcohol cabinet like a hawk, but they didn't have a clue of what was, or soon wasn't, in their medicine cabinet. And I would try anything.

And what's the use of changing your head, if you're not going to change your life?

So with my newfound lack of inhibition I started to interact with other people. The social pleasantries that had eluded me before were easily acquired. Sure, sometimes the conversations would end with puzzled looks on stranger's faces, but more often they ended okay. Sometimes they ended great. Great with balls on.

The shorter my dress, and the longer my buzz, the easier the interaction, and the better my nights started to end. From not liking anyone touching me I went to the other extreme. I would seek out a man's fingers and arms and mouth until I could feel every cell in my body alive with pleasure. All the things that my strange little head stopped me from feeling and playing with for so many long years burst open in front of me like a hedonistic playground.

Sure; there were times when I'd wake up with my head aching at the back and my tongue feeling like a piece of soiled carpet, but there was always a way to take it away again. There were times when I'd walk in at midday and my parents would yell and scream and threaten, but that only mattered if you listened and obeyed and I was past that. I was way past that.

There were times when I'd wake up next to someone with all the happy warm feelings drained out of my body and felt only revulsion at the thought of him touching me, having touched me. But that was just until I got my head right again.

My mother must have screamed at me a half dozen times before she gave up even trying about how I'd end up pregnant if I kept going like I was.

To give her credit when I told her, all shaking hands and acid stomach because I had stopped everything cold turkey as soon as I found out, she didn't say "I told you so." There was a look, of course there was a look, but I could handle that. It would have been the yelling and the recriminations that would've echoed in by hollowed out brain that would've lasted. My brain. My good old brain. Welcome home.

It was hard to be sober again. 1973 may not have been Woodstock in action like it was in other parts of the world, but we still had our fair share of free and easy loving and free and easy drugging. There were communes that soon collapsed but were started with hope and peace and love and without the stone-cold sobriety that I forced myself into for the benefit of the baby. My parents were different people than they had been the last time I had the wherewithal to examine them as people. I tried to tell myself that how they developed and how they'd grown was nothing to do with me, but it grew impossible not to attribute their weariness and caution and downtrodden slumped walk to my behaviour and their shame at how I'd turned out, and the guilt was a heavy burden to carry along with my own feelings of shame and disappointment and the growing burden inside my body.

There was a godsend that year. The government

decided to ruin the country by encouraging the promiscuous behaviour of its youth by paying them a benefit to have babies and stay at home without the benefit of getting married or having a man support them.

The disapproval was rife throughout the land, but it meant that once my baby was born I could finally move out of my parents' house and live on my own. In a tiny bedsit adjoining someone else's house sure, but at least I didn't have to walk past my own guilt every day.

My baby was quite good overall. A bit of a crier, but she settled down quickly enough after a feed and a cuddle. Plunket came to visit to give me help and advice, and I looked forward to the contact. Just as after being stuck with baby all day I looked forward to the trip to the dairy for essentials and the brief interaction with the couple who ran it.

I washed up thousands of reusable nappies; I washed up hundreds of baby clothes; I occasionally even got to spin my own blouses through the washing machine with their encrusted baby burps.

As baby grew older and started to crawl around the small floor space open to her, I started to venture further afield. I took her to the local park often, letting her crawl around on an old tartan rug in the sunshine, occasionally even watching her crawl off the edge and discover the wonderful world of grass, daisies and mud.

My mother began to visit more often, my father also sometimes tagging along. Although I still felt guilt when I saw my mum and dad, it was somewhat assuaged through watching them interact with their granddaughter and the pleasure she gave them. The pleasure I'd stopped being to them years before. As she visited more frequently I became used to relying on her for the odd spot of babysitting so I could go out and about without having to meticulously plan every step. I even found time to meet a nice man who was more than happy to escort me out to the odd meal, without expecting too much in return.

I fell into a new pattern. A good pattern. One where I had support and time with my baby and time without, *and someone who I felt I might have a future with.*

And then my mum died.

She and Dad had known for some time that she was ill, but hadn't wanted to trouble me with the knowledge. That was why she'd started to spend more time with her granddaughter. That was why she'd softened her attitude towards me. But not enough to let me in.

After her funeral, Dad was lost. He needed help to do anything, he needed meals cooked, and washing and ironing done, and to be called every weekday morning to be reminded to go to work. And then, just as I thought I might give up the bedsit and move back home to help him out he sold the house and decided to tour Europe with the funds.

So it was back to being just me and baby. The man I'd been seeing dropped out of sight; I'd never told him about my daughter – I didn't want to scare him off – and with no one to look after her anymore meeting up with him was no longer an option.

I missed him, well not him exactly but the intimacy of having a man in my life again, but I couldn't see a way to have that and keep my baby and stay on the benefit I needed to support us both. Unless a sugar daddy dropped out of the sky.

So it was back to the park, back to the quick trips to the dairy to catch a glimpse of adult life.

One morning in the park a woman was photographing the children and asked if she could take a few pictures of baby. Her accent was strange, she said she was Swedish, and she spoke in a sing song lilt. She sat beside me as she focused in on baby, and we chatted about the park and the day and the weather. We moved on to why she'd come out to New Zealand, and what she planned to do with her life, and where she was staying – an awful hostel that cost more money per night than I received in a week – and one thing led to another and she moved onto the couch.

I left baby with her the next day. I called up my man and told him I missed him and wanted to reconnect. He assured me he felt the same way and we made arrangements, and I talked with the Swede and she was happy to throw me a favour when I'd been so good as to let her into my home, and everyone was more than happy to fall in with my plans.

That was the last time I saw baby.

When I returned later that night the bedsit was empty. The pram was gone, so although I was surprised I wasn't really worried. They'd gone for a walk, they'd gone to the park, they'd taken advantage of the long summer evening to go for a stroll around the city and see all of the sights.

An hour after darkness fell I finally called the police. They came and took a statement, but assured me that they had probably just got caught up with something and would be on their way home soon. I could tell from the looks on their faces that it was nothing more than I deserved – all this worry after I'd left baby with a complete stranger. That's what you get.

Two days later they reluctantly started to mount searches, and put some effort into trying to locate my little girl. But there were no leads, there was no information. They didn't want me to appeal directly to the public because they might be put off by the tale of a hussy who'd got knocked up by a stranger when she was drugged out one night and then thought it was perfectly okay to live off of handouts instead of getting a job and then couldn't even be bothered to look after her child which was after all the only reason the state was paying me such a handsome sum to begin with. The country was going to rack and ruin and they didn't want me to appeal directly to the public because I was symptomatic of all that was wrong with society and that would just disengage everyone and they might actively try to work against the investigation rather than be of help.

I sat in the background, worried and guilty and scared. I first thought when they didn't come back that something terrible had happened to the Swede; that she'd been hurt and someone was looking after my baby until we were reunited. And I hoped that wouldn't be too long. That was what I had in the back of my mind when I went to the police. Then I grew angry. Obviously it wasn't an accident. Nothing bad had happened. The bitch I'd befriended had gone off on her own leaving my daughter at home all by herself and someone had nicked her. How dare she?

And then I finally caught up to where the police had started from. I'd taken in a mad stranger – a mad stranger from a foreign country who knew how to travel overseas all by herself – and I'd given her my daughter.

It was hard to take in the horror at what I'd done. It was hard to continue to live every single day with the guilt at how I'd let down baby with my own selfish needs. At the end I continued to live solely for the reason to apologise to her when she was found. Long years after I knew with my rational mind that I would never find my daughter I continued to phrase the words I would say, the thoughts I would try to express. Long after I should have accepted that even if she was still alive she wouldn't even know my name my face my relationship to her, and more probably she was dead, I would think of the mountains of shame I had to admit and lay bare in front of my baby – my one chance to present my sorrow.

And to this day when I fall asleep at night I think of her being raised in a far off country, with a beautiful woman that I didn't know who had loved her and supported her every day of her life.

My beautiful baby girl growing up happy.

CHAPTER TEN

I took Rena home, and called in a doctor I knew well from the days of my residency. Rena had avoided doctors due to fear of them trying to break her of her tendencies, and I didn't want to take her to the emergency department or a GPs office in this state.

After some quick consultation, Gavin gave her a sedative. It wasn't enough to send her to sleep, but it brought her rapid breathing and wild eye movements under control.

I'd left Ash at the scene. I'd been in too much of a hurry to get Rena out of there to think of his wellbeing also. I phoned his number to see if he'd managed to get away, but I couldn't get an answer. I tried to get hold of Erik, but the best I could manage was to leave a message saying I'd called.

'Could you go and get him for me? I want him here,' Rena pleaded when I went to see how she was doing. 'I don't want to be alone tonight. And he's the only one who'll understand what I went through today.'

So I drove back to the dive site.

There was far more people at the location than there had been when we left. Ash was among them, and Sarah Jones was sitting next to him. She sat with a rigid spine and her hands folded neatly in her lap. I felt a wave of distaste towards her. I understood that whatever was going on wasn't as a result of her actions, but she was irretrievably entwined with it in my mind.

'Ash,' I called out. I tried to be as quiet as I could, but heads turned all around.

Ash looked blankly at me.

I walked closer, and felt someone take my arm by the elbow and head me off before I got very far.

Erik leant his mouth down level with my ear. 'I need to talk to you alone.'

I nodded and allowed him to lead me over to a makeshift centre of operations consisting of a marquee, a pop-up tent and tarpaulin for a floor.

'Look, I can let you stay, but I really think it would be best if you took them both away from here. Is Mrs Sutherland okay?'

'Yes. There's a doctor friend of mine looking out for her at the moment, but she really wants Ash with her. I honestly thought he would have made it home under his own steam. Has he said why he wants to stay here?'

Erik looked out over the pond, and then back at me. His eyes were bloodshot, and the grey skies overhead were reflected in his skin tone.

'He wants to stay until all the bodies are found. He wants to make sure that Chloe isn't among them.'

'All the bodies?'

Erik sighed heavily and ran his right hand over his face.

'The dive team have located nine bodies so far. They are certain there are more.'

My mouth fell open with shock.

'Christine, I know I don't need to ask you to keep this under your hat, but I do need your help to make sure those two don't. The last thing I need tomorrow is going to be multiple bodies and a psychic fuelled media blitz.'

I tried to nod but my neck felt as though it was set in concrete. I tried to speak, but my mouth was to dry to function. I licked my lips and tried again.

'Yes. Yes I'll try to make sure they don't.'

I looked over to where they sat; their faces grimly observing all the movement around the pond.

I ran my tongue around inside my mouth to stimulate some saliva. 'Ash shouldn't be a problem. You still have a big stick you can wave at him if it comes to that. Sarah's the wild card. I can't imagine that this is something she's prepared to keep under her hat. She'll be trying to drum up business. Can't you try?'

Erik sighed. 'I've already explained the consequences. I've already asked her not to.' He shrugged his shoulders. 'I don't know that it had any effect at all. They both agree but they're looking completely blank. I can't get a read on her at all.'

I went back over and offered to drive Ash home so he could be with his ex-wife. He accepted, but Sarah refused the offer. She'd driven her own vehicle here so her arguments made too much sense to fight, and my head wasn't in a condition it could argue the point. I ferried Ash and then returned. If Sarah wasn't going to leave then at least I could stay and watch her watching them.

She stood resolute at the edge of the police tape. I thought that Erik could've done more, but he'd disappeared off, and it wasn't my place to interfere. There continued to be shouts and alerts from the dive site, even as the afternoon sun finally made an appearance through the grey cloud.

Erik's shoulders slumped more with each new signal, and he began to drink coffee after coffee as the afternoon turned into evening. I could sympathise. Every case that he'd grudgingly put aside so he could come out on this long shot was now relegated to his suspended file. These discoveries were about to occupy a lot of people for a lot of time.

There was a strange hypnotic mix of action/inaction, action/inaction. Halogen lights were brought in, and officers patrolled the perimeter of the tape, waiting for each new discovery. A flurry of activity, of views, and scribbles, and measurements, and photo relays. Then onto another wait.

I pulled up a chair next to Sarah. 'How're you doing?'

'I never thought...'

I waited for her to resume her sentence, but she stared blankly at the pond. The rosy light of the sunset reflected against the water's surface; a ripple of red.

'It's a lot to take in. Still, you must have known more than the rest of us.'

Sarah turned to face me, and I was appalled at how her skin had gone grey and strained tight like a years-old Christmas ornament.

'What?'

'You knew to bring the Sutherland's here. You must have known.'

'I didn't...'

'You did know. You told us exactly where to find this.'

'I mean I didn't know there'd be, be...' she waved her hand at the scene. 'I didn't know there'd be so many. I didn't know there'd be so much.'

I felt uneasy sitting there next to her. It was hard to take the years of anger and outrage that had been caused by people like Sarah coming in contact with my group. The harm and heartaches that followed in their wake like a slime-paved trail.

Hard to reconcile that with this small woman and her genuine gift.

Standing, I moved over to the edge of the tape closest to us. The screen was still set up over in the marquee but I couldn't view it from here. I could imagine they were documenting the position of everything and every new body in a process that would probably take the whole evening. There would be another shift coming on soon; even the police working a case had to have a chance to rest, but I couldn't imagine that Erik would leave any time soon. He was sipping another coffee as I watched him. The only fuel his body needs.

'I didn't mean to upset you the other day,' Sarah said quietly. When I turned back to her she was wringing her hands together in her lap. She had tiny, tiny hands.

'It wasn't my place to give you information. You hadn't asked for it, but it came through so strongly, I thought you deserved to know.'

'I don't understand,' I said as I sat down next to her again. 'What do you mean by "it came through so strongly"?'

'I don't understand it myself. But there was the image

in my head and I felt everything. And then it went away and I thought I should share it with you.'

'I don't believe in psychics. I don't believe you know the information you pretend to know.'

She turned to me and then slowly waved her hand over the full scene in front of us. 'This doesn't make you believe?'

'No. Tell me something about my daughter. If you're so great at knowing things you shouldn't be able to know, tell me something about Tamsin.'

'I've already....'

'No you haven't,' I interrupted. I was blunt and rude and I didn't care. 'You've told me that someone else was in the position I thought I'd seen my daughter in. Tell me something about her – not something about a stranger.'

'I can't call on it like that. I don't dictate the rules.'

'What did you see when you found out Chloe was here?'

I knew I was on dangerous ground. This was an area best left mined out from a police interrogation.

'I just felt her spirit. I felt her call to me.'

'And then what? She sent you a Google map reference?'

Sarah shrugged.

'The information was just there. I don't know any more than that.'

'But how was it there?' I persevered. 'Did you see co-ordinates? Did you see this landscape? Did you have a street number and name? Did you have a homing device set up? How was it there? How did you know this was here?'

I'd risen up in my seat and with the last question small drops of spit landed on Sarah's face.

She didn't flinch. She didn't lean back in her seat. She sat calmly with her eyes lowered, waiting for me to finish.

'Christine! What the fuck's going on here?'

Erik grabbed my shoulder from behind, and I shook him off and stood up and the chair fell backward and folded together with the quick change in movement. I stared a second as I tried to regain myself.

'I was just talking with Ms Jones.'

'The hell you were. I could hear you from across the field.'

'It's a very upsetting situation,' Sarah interjected.

'Yes. An upsetting situation that I've already requested you to leave once before, Ms Jones. Do you think this time you might actually be on your way?'

'I'd like to stay longer, if that's okay. I just want to make sure that Chloe's body is treated with respect.'

'It's not okay. And I don't know what your opinion of the police is Ms Jones, but we're not in the habit of being disrespectful to children's bodies. I'd like you to leave now.'

Sarah stood, and patted down the front of her dress her head tilted down. When she looked back up at Erik I could see the tight grip of desperation in her features.

'I'm sorry if I've disturbed your work. And I didn't mean to be insulting. I never thought for one moment that you would be anything other than professional. But I really need to stay. Please.'

'No, you'll be in the way. We've got to bring in a whole lot of equipment to try to dry this pond out so we can start to recover the bodies, and I don't need some laypeople hanging around getting in everybody's way.'

I had to admire how he'd managed to skilfully insert my dispatch from the scene into the same request.

'They won't be able to drain it.'

Both Erik and I turned abruptly at the note of certainty in Sarah's voice. She pointed at the camera feed.

'There's a constant ripple through the water. It's not being fed by the stream - it's being fed from a spring. You won't be able to drain it.'

'Another thing you just happened to know,' I said, voice heavy with sarcasm. But the fight had gone out of me. I was cold, tired, confused; and I didn't want to be sitting in the middle of a field fighting with a woman who already looked like she'd been beaten over and over again. 'Erik, you must know that she's involved with this somehow. You must know that.'

'Ms Jones would you kindly leave your address and

contact details with the sergeant over there,' he indicated a sole figure standing close to both our vehicles. 'Then you can be on your way.'

'I'm afraid I can't do that. You don't have the right to ask.'

I turned to her in astonishment. I understood her refusing to answer my questions – I wasn't in the most rational mood right at the moment – but was she really refusing a query from the police?

'You will do that, or I'll place you under arrest and have one of my officer's escort you back to the station for interview.'

'She forgives you,' Sarah suddenly blurted, looking straight at me.

Both Erik and I turned to look at her, but her gaze was unfocused and her head tilted to one side. A small line of drool tracked down the crease next to her mouth.

'What the hell. Lady, you can give your details as I've directed or I'm forcefully removing you right now,' Erik announced, but I put a restraining hand on his arm.

'She knows that you were holding on to her so tight. She felt you cradling her even as the water closed in overhead. That was her last thought. Mummy's holding on to me, I'll be safe. Mummy's holding on to me so tight. She knows it wasn't your fault. She knows you tried your best to keep her safe.'

I stared at Sarah as I felt hot bile rising in my throat.

'Christine. Are you...?'

I was around the side of the tent running to make sure I was past the tape, then sprawling on the muddy ground as I threw up, and threw up again. Hot tears of pain and anger squeezed out as another clench voided my stomach and left foul acid coating the inside of my mouth. How could she? How dare she?

I retched again, but there was nothing left to come up. I pushed myself to my feet and wiped my mouth with the back of my hand. I felt dizzy and my ears were buzzing like I'd just been on an eight-hour plane ride. My head felt full and hot.

When Erik's hand came down on my shoulder it felt like a cool flannel against my hot skin.

'She's gone, Christine. You don't need to worry about her.'

'Gone where?'

'We've taken her into custody.'

He didn't owe me that much, but I was grateful that he told me.

'You know there's no such thing as psychics, don't you?' his voice continued.

I nodded. I nodded, but my mind was crawling over details, crawling over memories, wriggling and scurrying through the deep dark places that I pretended didn't exist.

Yes I knew there was no such thing as a psychic. Even if I'd waivered for a moment, this encounter had just firmly planted the knowledge back in me. It didn't make the "revelations" any easier to deal with.

'Are you okay to make it back home?'

I nodded again, and turned back to see how far it was to my car. Of course I'd be fine. I was always fine.

I turned back and retched again.

***

I drove around for a while after leaving the pond. When I first got into my vehicle I thought I would head straight home. I was so tired that it wasn't safe for me to drive, and I could think of nothing better than going home, going straight up to bed, and going straight to sleep.

The thought of another run-in with Gary made me pause. I wouldn't be able to deal with anymore drama; and with his history in mind drama was likely to be there after his most recent behaviour.

So I drove around and around, hoping that I would find the courage to go home, or the conviction to do something else, and instead found nothing.

In the end I parked up near the top of Balmoral Hill, looking out over the sea view.

Gary and I had a place here before we left for Thailand. The new owners had reshaped the house, reshaped the section, put in a swimming pool, knocked out walls and knocked up a new level.

As a reward they'd had a good six months to enjoy the spot before the February 2011 earthquake decided to do some remodelling of its own.

The section was now empty. The house was removed in full before it could drop onto the land at the base of the hill; some of which contained a primary school with a sign relabeling it as Danger High. It would've worked so much better with a high school, but at least the locals were trying to look on the bright side.

There was a clear view out over the estuary and then further out to sea. Dots on the horizon denoted the location of ships; most likely cargo vessels but there were occasional cruise ships pulling around the heads to make a shore stop in Lyttelton.

The persistent drizzle had finally given up and only a smatter of clouds was now visible across the sky. The moon was almost full; the light reflecting in the ocean in a shaky beam toward the horizon.

I tried closing my eyes. Falling asleep in the car may be uncomfortable, but the relief from consciousness would be appreciated more than the physical pain could detract. It was no use though; my mind was processing too much information to let my body rest.

Nine bodies. Nine people thrown into a pond in the middle of nowhere and no one had even noticed. Nine, at least, I amended.

I sat and I stared. I stared and I sat.

When the first colour of morning started to show on the horizon I turned the key and started the drive back home. By this time Gary should either be unconscious or grumpily awake and hungover. Either way it was better than drunk and talkative.

As I let myself in I couldn't hear Gary about. If he'd fallen asleep downstairs there would've been the clear sound of snoring coming from the couch, but there was nothing.

I crept up the stairs, but still couldn't hear any sounds.

Grateful for the lack of contact I lay down on the bed fully clothed. There was no disturbance to the covers so

Gary must have crashed somewhere else.

That was the last thought I had had from the most horrible day.

***

Erik called me at midday and woke me from a deep sleep.

'You still in contact with that Kendra Little woman?' he barked.

I sat up in bed and pulled a couple of lumps of sleep from my eye. My brain took a few seconds to compute the question.

'You know my group is protected by privilege.'

'Yes I know.'

I shook my head to clear it. Sleep had eluded me for much of the night, but when I'd finally fallen it kept a firm grip.

'It's just a question Christine. We can try other avenues if it's breaking some code.'

'Yes I'm still in contact. Why?'

'She had a kid reported missing in 1974. That sound familiar?'

'Yes.' I rubbed my hand over my face and shook my head. 'Her babysitter abducted her when she went out for the night. She didn't know her well – met her in the park.'

'That's the one. Her babysitter was Swedish right?'

I tried to remember the last time Kendra had spoken. She'd been going to group so long that she didn't often tell her story. Lots of advice but little input.

'That sounds about right. Why?'

'It's one of the few cases we have on the books where there's a missing child and the case isn't solved.'

'But it is solved. The babysitter...'

'The babysitter is missing along with the girl. No trace of either of them.'

'Yeah, but she probably would've gone back to Europe. Kendra didn't even know her full name so they couldn't trace her, but there was no order stopping her moving about. You didn't even need a full passport for a child in those days – they were just an endorsement, if that.'

Erik's sigh let me know clearly that I'd disappointed him. I was used to it though. Water, ducks, blah, blah, blah.

'That may be what they thought at the time, but on the books it's unsolved. I need to bring her in.'

'So bring her in.'

'She hung up on me. She refused to open her door to the officer I sent around.'

I wanted to laugh, but I stemmed the urge. I could imagine Kendra giving him and his mates short shrift. Even if he'd remembered to be polite for once.

'I don't know if it's in her file or not, but she was treated abominably by the police the first time around. They basically wrote her off as a whore who gave her daughter away.' I paused in thought. 'Do you really think one of those bodies belongs to her daughter? It was forty years ago.'

'So far we don't have any timeline so all possibilities need to be looked at. We just need a DNA sample. For comparison. It'll only take fifteen minutes out of her day.'

'If you don't even think one of those bodies belongs to her daughter I really advise against it.'

'Well, what the hell else are we to do? We've got twelve new unsolved murders on the books – nine of them children – and absolutely no idea of where to start.'

I sat in silence while the numbers stormed through my head.

'Twelve?'

Erik paused. I presumed he'd remembered he wasn't speaking to a sworn officer and perhaps revealing information to the public wasn't the best of ideas.

'You didn't hear it from me.'

'Is there anything else I didn't hear from you?'

I was appalled and fascinated at the same time. How could nine children end up in a pond – that close to a major city – and no one ever be the wiser? Forget the adults. Nine children. No wonder Erik was scrambling through his cold case file.

'She won't come in alone and I think that's fair. I

want either me or a lawyer to accompany her, and make sure you and everyone in your station room is on their best behaviour, all right? If you stuff this one up you're not going to get another chance.'

'We're trying to solve a crime here Christine. We'll get as many chances as we need to.'

'She's hurt and angry. You push her and you'll be taking your samples on sixty minutes.'

'It's not on TV anymore.'

I didn't respond. I knew from experience you could always outwait pedantry.

'Fine. Whatever. You know so much better than us professionals after all.'

'I'll call in to hers this morning,' I checked my watch and corrected myself, 'this afternoon, and I'll try to convince her to come in today, but Detective Senior Sergeant?'

'Yes?'

'I'm serious about the kid gloves. If you don't treat her with the utmost respect she'll just refuse to deal with you at all. If you need her cooperation you need to treat her nicely.'

'Like a little lamb, Christine. Just get something off her. We're scrambling.'

'Is twelve the final total?'

'Looks like it. There's some kind of internal spring feeding the pond.'

I pursed my lips together. 'Like Sarah said last night,' I interrupted. There was a long silence and then Erik continued as though I hadn't made a sound.

'It feeds in and then it sucks it back down. There were bones found near the part where it goes back under. They can't form whole skeletons from them so the presumption is there could've been more than we've pieced together so far.'

'Where does it end up?'

'What?' The abrupt query silenced me for a second. But you have to forgive someone under stress, don't you?

'If there's a spring feeding it, and then a channel sucking it back down, where does it end up? It must come out somewhere.'

'Yes, it must come out somewhere. Some guy from NIWA chucked a bunch of stuff in there, tagged and GPS'd up the wazoo. It moved but it hasn't emerged anywhere, and he lost the signal when it went too deep.'

He laughed abruptly, and I was startled by the change in tone. But if there was anything that Erik appreciated it was the culpability of another government department in having to justify its outrageous spending.

'They've got people stationed at a couple dozen different sites where they think these things might show up. I've love to see their expense report. Wait until the media gets hold of that one.'

'Has the media got wind of it yet?'

'Not a peep so far. We've locked down the station as much as we can; if we can buy just another day or two it will give us a hell of an advantage. Even just till the end of the day.'

'What about Sarah? Is she talking to the media?'

Erik paused, then 'I'm not at liberty to say.'

Good. She was still in custody then.

I was still dressed in clothes from yesterday and pulled them off as I walked down the hall to the bathroom. The hood from my top was still damp from the rain, but the rest seemed to have dried on my body as I slept.

I forced them into the laundry hamper beside the bathroom door as I walked through. I really should get around to washing those someday, but I doubted today would be the day.

There was a metallic smell in the air, but I didn't really connect to it until I pulled back the shower curtain. There was no reason for it to be pulled across. We left it back when the shower was empty, mainly because I thought it was too much like Psycho when it was closed.

There was deep red staining all across the wall. In a spray pattern that reached all the way to the ceiling. My eyes tracked it up while my brain tried to forget what it had just seen in the tub.

My legs gave way under me as my arms fell limp to my side. The curtain fell back into place, hiding the view to the tub.

I tried to kneel, but everything was shaking and useless. I tried to open my mouth to yell for help but I couldn't make a sound.

I remembered when Gary and I had been in high-school. He'd pulled the ring-tab off a can of lemonade and put it on my finger. It had taken him another five years, but eventually he'd replaced it was a small diamond. The ring-tab was still in my jewellery box.

I tried again and managed to get my legs under me in a sitting position. I pulled back the curtain again, hard, and then pushed it further so that when I let it go it stayed out of the way.

Gary lay in the tub. There was a razor dropped from his lifeless fingers, and blood pooling around his groin.

It was so like Martin Hinks that I wondered for a moment if I were dreaming. Was I going to see a severed body part if I leant forward?

I wasn't.

Gary had slit through his femoral artery. I had no idea when, but I could see that blood was still pumping out.

Blood was still pumping out.

He was alive.

Adrenalin energised my body, and I stood and ran to the medicine cabinet. There was a huge stockpile of bandages there. I grabbed a handful and shoved them into Gary's crotch. Hard against the inside of his thigh. I tied it off with yet another bandage. Not tight to form a tourniquet, but enough to keep on the pressure.

My phone? Where had I put my phone?

I was halfway back to the bedroom when I discovered it in my pocket. I left it and kept going to the landline in the hall. They'd be able to trace it back if I needed to drop the line.

'Fire, Ambulance, Police?'

My mind went blank for a moment. I wanted to say Police.

'Ambulance. I need an ambulance.'

I was patched through to another line and I blurted it out again.

'What's the nature of the injury?'

'Cut. My husband's cut himself.'

I dropped the phone and ran back to the bathroom. There was still blood seeping through the bandages. I pressed my fingers hard against the side of Gary's neck and recognised the beat of his pulse. I ran back to the phone.

'He's cut through an artery,' I barked into the line without even checking to see that someone was there. 'He's lost a lot of blood, but he's still alive.'

I heard acknowledgement and dropped the phone again. I ran downstairs and opened the front door then turned and ran back to the bathroom. The crew would be able to hear me, and they would save time if they didn't have to break the door open.

'Gary. Gary can you hear me?'

His eyelids fluttered. Once. Twice. He opened his eyes and focused on my face and smiled. Then he closed them again.

I felt for his pulse, and kept my fingers on it this time. It was still beating when I heard the crew downstairs and yelled out my location. It was still beating as they levered him out of the bath and rushed him into the back of the ambulance. It was still beating when we arrived at the hospital, and still beating when two men physically pulled me away from my husband.

Still beating.

CHAPTER ELEVEN

Denise's Story

From the moment I was old enough to know that there were careers and jobs and choices that people can make that lets them decide what they do each and every day of their life, I knew I wanted to be a dancer.

It wasn't the tutus, although they were awesome. It wasn't the beautiful satin of the tiny shoes with the hard backbone to support your weight en pointe, although they were cool. It wasn't the complicated steps and movements and the grace with which they choreographed them together to show a flow that made you see things that weren't there, although that was magic.

It was the line of the body.

The smooth design that I could see when I bent and twisted and stepped and swooped and turned and leaned and flew.

The line of my body writing a story upon the stage.

There were other people in my ballet class who were leaner, lither, taller, lighter, but they were playing at the dance. They weren't living it like I was.

I was slightly heavier than I needed to be, but from

the age of eight I learned that what you put in your body affects how much you weigh, and I counted calories and grams of protein and fat from that moment on. No need to count carbs as they weren't going near my mouth.

I trimmed down and toned up and I made sure I stayed that way. If I had to work harder at it than the other girls then that was the sacrifice demanded of any dreamer. This was the test of my stamina.

When my breasts started to grow I taped them up. There was no place for cleavage on the stage; no place for the curve of a hip. I watched my diet more and more. I employed more and more tricks and tips to keep my weight where it should be. Every morning I damned my gender that it should want to store body fat – BODY FAT – as some old-age internal mechanism of my species.

Survival be damned; I was going to be the size I wanted and there was no one who was going to stop me.

I don't remember a lot about the night it happened. The night I "became a woman." In truth I think it's better that way.

When I do think about it, which is more often than I'd like, I remember disgust at the thought of something extra inside me. I tried so hard to keep my body pure from food and drink and now there was another orifice receiving input. Another drop or two of weight to flush like a toxin from by body.

There'd been a glass of wine. To this day I don't know if there was anything else inserted; a "mickey" slipped in there, or whether it was just the effect of alcohol on a body system that took in almost no calories.

A month or two later I noticed that I couldn't shed weight the way I used to. No matter the amount of abstention I was putting on a pound here, a pound there.

I worked harder. I drove myself further. I cut down to the barest of essentials, and then cut it down further. I wasn't going to allow whatever fresh hell this was to determine my size and shape. I was in control. I was control.

By the time I worked out that it wasn't my body betraying me but an alien life form hitching a ride it was too late.

Terminations are only possible with two doctors signing off on them, and only within the first three months. I tried to fight with the doctors and point out that it was a threat to my life to continue with the pregnancy, but they weren't interested. They wouldn't listen.

At night I would fall asleep dreaming of knitting needles, gin and a hot bath, long flights of slippery stairs.

During the day I ignored my situation. I tried to continue on as I had been.

My abdominal muscles were so tight from years of dance that even though the weight continued to climb there was no obvious physical sign. When I pressed against my lower stomach there was absolutely no give anymore. If it had been due to muscle mass I would've been ecstatic.

There was an opening on a dance troupe tour. In prior years I would've turned up my nose at the opportunity. In prior years I was keeping myself clean and ready for the big time. In prior years I had more options.

I toured around the country as my weight grew higher and my body grew harder. The line of my body finally started to give way to the inevitability of its on-board hitchhiker, but there was only gossip about my lack of control. Superior looks and raised eyebrows in the change room.

When the tour was finished I didn't tell my family. I continued to write and phone as though I was in a different centre every night. I continued to "tour" for another three weeks while I stayed in parts of Christchurch that I'd never dreamed existed. Parts of Christchurch that I didn't want to know.

Everything that I'd put off for so long started to return home to roost. I couldn't think with the panic;

couldn't think with the horror that was soon to befall me. And then I met him.

In a seedy backstreet market where I shopped for food; that sold horsemeat as pet food that everybody accepted would end up in hamburgers. He took an interest and he offered a life-line and I jumped.

When I gave birth to my freeloader it was quick and easy. The strong muscles that had been toned over years of use, that had hidden my pregnancy from view, they popped the alien right out of me quick smart.

I stayed overnight, pretending to have trouble breast-feeding so I wouldn't have it latching onto me. Being given machinery to pull the lactation from my breasts – my fat, fat, fat breasts.

And then I took the parasite and fled down the fire escape.

He met me in the hospital car park. I handed the bundle over and walked away and never thought about it again. Never crossed my mind as I worked to get back to where I had been. Poised on the edge of everything I'd worked so hard for so many years to achieve.

When the police came I genuinely didn't know what they were talking about.

They were querying a birth and a hospital and a baby that couldn't be accounted for. It was six years later, and I genuinely didn't know what they were talking about.

I told them one story to get them off my back, but they came again and again and again until I told them the truth.

And they didn't believe me.

I was signed on to the trainee programme with the New Zealand Royal Ballet. I finally had everything in my grasp.

And they didn't believe me.

I thought it would go away. Can you believe that? There was a time when I actually believed that they would just go away. The police would stop calling on me, stop questioning me, stop recommending that I retain a lawyer – a lawyer for God's sake – and just fade into the background.

In the end it was the Crown Prosecutors who decided to press ahead with the charges of murder. The police had decided that there was no evidence of a body, no evidence of an act of murder, and therefore there could be no successful prosecution, and then they were overridden by the Crown Prosecution Service.

What does CPS stand for?

Couldn't prosecute Satan.

But they could prosecute me.

I couldn't defend myself. I talked it over with the lawyer I'd finally been forced to retain, and I explained over and over exactly what had happened, but he decided that it might be a bad idea to put my evidence before the jury.

For a long time I wouldn't accept it. I thought that if I just stood there and told everybody exactly what had happened it would all make sense to them and the whole thing would finally go away.

He mocked up a trial situation and cross examined me.

It wasn't pretty.

So we went in there with a motion to dismiss due to lack of evidence – they didn't even have a body for Christ sake. Let alone a murder weapon. But they thought they had enough and the judge agreed.

A birth, and then an absence. Something and then nothing. That was their case. It was pathetic.

Okay, looking back perhaps handing a child to a virtual stranger in a car park wasn't the most motherly thing in the world, but I hadn't killed it.

I was certain right up until the verdict that my complete innocence would actually work in my favour. That the jury would look at this rubbish case they'd fabricated and see the truth – that I hadn't committed murder. That I hadn't done anything wrong. People gave their babies away every day for adoption. Okay, I hadn't gone through the right channels but seriously? Murder?

Someone on the jury agreed with me.

If this had been the good old days that would've been enough to keep me free. I could've gone on my merry way and resumed my career, my life.

But this isn't the good old days.

A majority verdict was accepted and I was convicted of a murder that I didn't commit.

My lawyer says there are grounds for appeal. Lots of grounds for appeal.

But what does that matter?

It will take years to have even a first appeal and by that time my chance will be gone. What would I have to go back to in two-three years' time? A career as a dance instructor?

I'd rather rot in here.

They stole my life.

CHAPTER TWELVE

I don't know how long I'd been at the hospital before Kendra turned up to join me. I hadn't called her. Stevie phoned my mobile to find out where I was and I bluntly told her. I didn't pay too much attention to what I was saying at the time but it must've been bad enough that she'd taken it upon herself to phone someone to come and sit with me.

It was hard not to be doing something. My mind had a thousand memories playing all at the same time. Every night since I'd met Gary, every day we'd spent together – or apart. Crowded thoughts. It kept the full horror of sitting in a waiting room expecting at any moment that someone would come in and tell me my husband was dead at bay.

Instead they told me the opposite.

Gary was still unconscious when they let me see him, but the doctor reassured me that his vital signs were good, and he should wake up naturally by the end of the day. I sat at his bedside for another hour or so, and then came back out to find Kendra was still waiting for me.

'I'm getting myself a cup of coffee,' Kendra said in a surprisingly nice tone considering I'd ignored her since she arrived. 'Can I get you anything?'

I started to shake my head, but then I followed her to the door. 'I'll come with you.' I needed to move about and try to focus on something different.

'Do you want to grab lunch?' she asked as we walked to the cafeteria. 'You mustn't have had time to eat anything.'

I shook my head no, but when I got to the café I put a few bits and pieces on a plate. Habit, or my body telling me it needed fuel no matter what my mind thought.

As I bit into a cheese scone, and wished I'd gone for the offer of butter, I remembered there was something I needed to talk to Kendra about. Erik had phoned, I thought. It seemed so long ago.

'I have something to ask you,' I began, and then felt guilty as Kendra leant forward her face full of concern and sympathy. 'Not about Gary,' I added, and she sat back.

'What about, then?'

'DSS Smith phoned me this morning and said that he'd tried to talk to you.'

Kendra's face turned into a mask, and she froze in the act of stirring her coffee.

'He asked me to ask you if you would be able to come in to the station.'

Kendra's face was set, and she put her hand up.

'I'm not going in there.'

'Did he tell you why?'

'He said they were taking another look at my daughter's case. As though they took a look in the first place. I told him no. It's not as though anything is going to be found this far down the track.'

'I mean, did he explain why they're reopening it?'

Kendra put her coffee cup down on the table. She wiped away the small lipstick smear from the side of the porcelain.

'There was a discovery made yesterday.' I began, then stopped as I didn't know how to continue. My mind was weary from horror piled on top of horror. The last two days felt like they were too much to cope with. Or would be too much. When my mind came back to itself enough to start trying to cope with anything.

'Have they found a body?' Kendra asked. Her voice was so quiet I struggled to make it out over the background hum of the café.

'They've found a lot of bodies,' I responded. 'He doesn't know if there's any connection with your daughter at all, but he's going through all of the possible cases that they still have on the books.'

I put my hand on the back of Kendra's and waited until she looked up.

'He would like you to come in and give a DNA sample. It will be very quick. The sample is just a swab from the inside of your mouth so will take only a minute or two to collect.'

'How do you know this? Why is he telling you?'

'There was a tip-off in the Sutherland case. They were out at the site and I was there as support for them when they found the first body.'

'Was it their little girl?'

I shook my head. 'They don't know yet. They won't know until they've matched results. Rena couldn't identify her from the clothing, but...' I shrugged the rest of the explanation.

'Do you really think my daughter could be involved?'

I shrugged again. 'I don't know. It's possible otherwise they wouldn't ask. Ilene's probably been asked to come in to. Maybe we could all go in together.'

'But the babysitter...'

I took a deep breath, and hoped that Erik wouldn't mind the information exchange if it got him what he needed.

'They found the remains of nine children and three adults. It's possible that one of them may be your daughter. It's possible that one may be your babysitter.'

Kendra stared at my face for a long time. I don't know what she was trying to read there, or even if it was me that she was really seeing. I tried to stay still and give her time.

'They could both have been murdered?' She asked finally. She picked up her coffee again and drained it in one long pull.

'I don't know Kendra, but it could be possible.'

Her hands gripped the empty cup between them, her fingers interlocked. I watched as her grip tightened, the skin turning white with strain.

'They said it was my fault,' she said. Her voice had once again become quiet. 'They said that woman was probably after her all along and I'd just handed my little girl over to her.'

I nodded. I understood the thought process behind this assessment, at the same time that I understood what that implied about Kendra.

'But if they were both taken. If they were both murdered...'

She trailed off, and looked out the side window at the people walking along on a beautiful sun-filled day. Their shadows were beginning to lengthen as the midday turned to mid-afternoon.

She didn't need to finish the sentence. I knew what it implied also.

If they'd both been taken, and both been murdered, then maybe it wasn't Kendra's fault.

She'd lived with guilt for almost forty years, and now there was another option.

'Would you come in with me? I don't want to go by myself.'

'Of course I will. I'd be glad to.'

There was a sharp sound as the mug succumbed to the pressure and cracked in Kendra's hands.

***

'Rena's holding up okay, but I think she's more worried that the police will just stop looking for Chloe now that they've opened a new case. It had pretty much stalled anyway – that was why that did that appalling article to begin with.'

I shifted my weight from one butt cheek to the next. When I'd first sat down next to Gary's bed the seat had been perfectly comfortable, but as the minutes turned to hours it became ever less so. I alternated from one side to another, and then stood until my legs started to complain, then sat again.

'Kendra needs to go back into the station again. Erik very kindly called her directly to request her attendance.'

I laughed. 'At least that's how she said he put it. I'll go in and hold her hand. I hope it's good news. Good news for her – either way.'

Gary stared straight ahead. It was hard to tell just by looking that he'd emerged from the coma. He was unresponsive. There wasn't even a flinch from pain-provoking activities such as changing his catheter bag or adding another line for a drip.

He'd been moved out of the hospital. If he'd been hurt in an accident he would've been in a general ward, close to being released.

Due to his circumstances he was on a three-day hold at the psychiatric hospital. If he didn't show any signs of responsiveness soon then it would be extended at the end of the compulsory admittance period.

I sighed and shifted my weight again.

'Erik also wants me to go out to the prison with him today. I asked him if Stevie or another volunteer could go in my place, but he wasn't keen. It felt wrong to say no.' I didn't know why that was, but it was true. He was the only person in my life that was fully stable right now. I could always count on him to be an annoying prick only concerned with himself and his focus and this was holding true.

'It's to meet with a woman they're holding there for murder. Turns out she wasn't involved in her baby's death at all. Isn't that awful? She's been locked up in prison and the whole time her baby was dead at the bottom of a pond. Her whole unbelievable testimony turned out to be true.'

I left soon after. A nurse had raised Gary's arm into the air to allow easier access when she checked his drip. It remained there – like an invisible puppeteer held the string. I placed it back on the covers, and left the room.

At the prison I clutched the approved visitors form in my hand as I locked up the car. Double beeps then I checked the handles to be sure. Not that I was drawing conclusions just because of the location.

There was a group of twenty people in the waiting room already as I handed over my documentation to the reception officer. When I explained who I was meeting I thought there would be a fast-track through a different system. Instead I received a wristband and was told to take a plastic seat to wait. Another six people joined us in the room before a horn sounded in the background, and people started to get waved through.

A detour followed where an officer patted me down thoroughly, under clothing but over underwear. A quick shake through my hair and I was through.

My phone buzzed with an incoming message as I walked through into the visitor's area. Erik was caught up with something else. Another officer was on his way. I should wait until he arrived.

Whatever.

Tables were packed closely in the room, and there were family and friends seated around them. Prisoners in their bright orange overalls were dotted about the place.

It had been a long time since I'd been in a prison, and then only in a medical capacity. I'd forgotten how claustrophobic it felt, even with the attempt at a casual atmosphere.

There were booths in another room, and although they felt even worse, closed in and restricted, I wondered as soon as I sat if it wouldn't have been a better idea. The room was loud with the hum of a dozen different conversations, some of them already husky with emotion.

Denise Jacobs may have been locked inside for a long period of time, but she looked very much the same as the photo I'd seen on her file. She was rod thin. The legacy of her years as a dancer still holding her firmly in control of her weight, but she'd escaped the scrawny face that so often accompanied long term weight control.

She was angry.

From the moment she walked into the room I could see the emotion boiling off her skin.

Denise sat opposite me, her hands clasped together with such force that the skin shone white.

'What's this about?' she asked.

'I wanted to see you to talk about the disappearance of your daughter.'

'The warden said. What about her?'

'The police may have discovered her body.'

'What do you mean the police? Aren't you the police?'

'I'm with victim support. I'm here to help you with anything you may need. There should be a police officer here shortly.'

I shouldn't have been saying anything. It was wrong. But I couldn't take back what I'd already said, and I wanted to see her reaction. It wasn't fair to let her suffer in this place any longer. 'He'll tell you the same thing. They've discovered a body.'

Denise frowned; the line cut a sharp crease in her forehead. It was an odd contrast to the youth of the rest of her face.

She shook her head. 'I don't know what you mean. I didn't kill her you know. I've been set-up. Someone set me up.'

I nodded in agreement. 'I believe you.'

'Then how have you found a body? She's not dead. Where did you find her?'

The questions tumbled out on top of each other. Denise didn't even seem to realise they contradicted one another.

'We don't know that it's her for sure. We do have a match on her mitochondrial DNA.'

'What's that,' Denise interjected.

'It shows that she's a familial relative of yours. She could be a sibling or a daughter.'

Denise stared at me for a long time. She opened her mouth to speak, and then closed it shut again.

I waited. I didn't want to interject anything that would ruin her chance to absorb the information. I could always come back.

She pulled her hands into her lap, and stared at them. As if they were a magic eight ball that would give her an answer she could heed.

'There was more than one.'

I sat back in shock. Nothing was in her file, and nothing had come out during the court case.

'Before or after?'

'After. I took birth control but it just never seemed to

take. My GP always used to say that I'd have trouble conceiving if I kept starving myself the way I was, but he was full of crap.'

She looked from her hands back up to me. There was a pull to the corner of her mouth that showed obstinacy. There was nothing to indicate any pain or regret.

'Whereabouts did you give birth?'

She looked down at her hands again. 'I went out on the road again. I couldn't dance for as long the second time, I knew that I wouldn't be able to, so I put money aside.'

She shook her head side to side. 'I didn't want to take time off, not again, not so soon after the last time. I didn't go to a hospital. I was in a house that I rented in Rangiora. It was cheap and no one knew who I was. I put food away so I wouldn't have to leave the house when I grew so large there couldn't be any doubt I was pregnant. I gave birth in the house. He was early.'

I held her gaze when she looked up this time and reached my hand out to her. 'That must have been hard. It must have been frightening.'

She shook her head slightly and turned to look over at another table where two small children were playing under the table while their parents ignored them.

'He was dead from the beginning. I was only thirty weeks gone. He came out after only a few hours. He was tiny. He was blue. I buried him in the back garden.'

She calmly turned to look at me again. 'I'm glad you've found his body. It never set right with me leaving him there like that. I wanted to do more for him, but I left it all too late.'

It was hard to take everything in. It was hard to believe her words when they came from a face that had calmed into stillness. Absent emotion.

She gave a short laugh. 'I was terrified that he'd be found when I was on trial. I was terrified they'd find him and say "see, she let her boy die of course she killed her baby girl as well", but I needn't have worried about that, eh.'

I cleared my throat. 'The police have found the body of a small female child. She was found in a location just outside of Christchurch, in a pond; I can't disclose the exact location at the moment. The body appears to be 3-4 years old by the pathologist's examination, and we have a mitochondrial DNA match to you.'

Denise stared at me for long moments, her face completely blank. Then the corner of her mouth turned up in an ironic smile at the same time as her eyes teared up.

'Well, shit. I should've checked before I opened my mouth shouldn't I?' She wiped a tear away when it threatened to fall from the corner of her eye, and laughed. 'Although I suppose they can't do much more to me can they? Maybe a concurrent sentence?'

Denise tipped her head forward and put her hands over her face. She sat for a few minutes, not a single muscle moving, then put them down into her lap again, her face once again composed.

'How could my daughter be in a pond? Where was her father?'

I looked at her long and hard and I felt the final tug of belief.

'I don't know. I don't know how she came to be there. We'll want to find out more about her father though. I imagine he may be a very strong lead.'

Denise frowned at me. 'But you're not even police, are you?'

'No, I'm not. I've just been referred by them so that you have support if you want it.'

Denise sat back in her chair and stared at the family next to us again. She continued to look at them as she slowly spoke her next sentence.

'So this isn't a formal interview? You can't use any of what I just said to you in a court of law?'

I leaned across the table and reached out for her hand. There was a second of hesitation and then Denise laid hers in mine.

'As far as the police know I'm waiting for them out in the public area. You can tell me anything and I won't be obliged to pass it on.'

'Was she alone? Was my baby girl out there all alone?'

I shook my head.

'There were others?'

I nodded, and felt her withdraw her hand from mine.

'How many?'

'I can't really tell you that.'

She cocked her head to the side and looked me full in the face. 'You can you know. I'm not obliged to pass any information on to the police either.'

I smiled, and nodded. 'Twelve bodies so far. Nine of them are children.'

'Bullshit. There's nothing on the news.'

'There probably will be soon. The media haven't yet found out, and until the police have some lead on what's going on they're happy to leave them in the dark. The only people being contacted are those who may be affected.'

'Like me?'

I nodded again.

'Could this end with me getting out of here?'

I shrugged. 'It should. I can't see your charges sticking if they can prove that the body is your daughter, and that you had nothing to do with her death.'

'I've been in here since two years after she was born,' Denise retorted. 'From what you say she was still alive when I was locked up.'

I nodded at her.

'I always thought that she'd be found one day. She'd be found and I'd be let out of here.' A tear rolled down her cheek and she wiped it away with the back of her hand. She tried to smile. 'I just thought she'd be alive when it happened.'

***

I waited with Kendra while the police faffed about looking for the right person. To deliver what news we didn't know, but it had been made clear that we were summoned on urgent business and we were to stay until it was finished.

Kendra paced the lobby. She came too close to a suspect being half-walked, half-dragged in through the front doors and he tried vaguely to head butt her. She laughed shrilly at the diversion and went back to pacing.

We waited so long that I scrolled through the list of contacts on my phone and tried calling Erik on his direct line to find out what was going on, but he didn't answer.

I found out why when he finally stormed through the door a good half-hour later.

'Goddamn interview took hours,' he snarled in greeting and took off again without bothering to explain where we were going. 'Woman wouldn't stop talking. Kept her silence for too bloody long that one, and now you can't shut her up.'

'What's this about?' I asked as it was apparent he wasn't about to tell us.

'Eh? Didn't they tell you?'

'I wouldn't be asking if they had.'

'Yeah, well. We're nearly there now.'

'Do I need a solicitor?' Kendra asked in a quiet voice from next to me.

'Shouldn't think so. Nothing like that going on.'

He pushed through into an empty room and I was startled to see it was one of the two rape suites in the building. They were furnished in the fashion of a normal lounge room rather than looking like an interview room. Theory being that a victim would feel more like dispensing a full and frank account of the brutal attacks they'd been subjected to if they weren't in a small concrete cell with a wooden table and a plastic chair and two officers, everybody in the room wishing they didn't have to be there.

It made me more nervous to be in there, rather than more comforting. Softly, softly room meant there was something bad coming our way.

'Right, well this is about the DNA you submitted to the inquiry,' Erik began.

Kendra jerked backwards in her chair, her face white.

'I thought you didn't have a match?' I asked. I think more to give us both a breathing space, rather than to try to contradict the news that Erik was about to give Kendra.

'We didn't find a match in the bodies we retrieved.'

Erik confirmed, an answer that surprised me even more.

'My daughter's alive?' Kendra questioned. She leaned forward in her chair, her face still with anticipation.

I grabbed and held her hand as I waited for the denial I knew would follow.

'Yes, she is,' Erik, flooring me completely.

'Tell you the truth,' he continued, 'we're not sure of your rights with this one. We don't think we're allowed to tell you the identity of your daughter as she's now an adult and there is no one holding her against her will. I do want to ask your permission to pass on your details to her so she can make a decision as to whether or not she meets you. But I can confirm that she's still alive.'

Kendra was shaking with emotion. Her face was streaming tears while her chest was heaving with laughter.

Erik looked away so he didn't have to deal with it. I placed a hand on her back and rubbed up and down briskly. What was the right reaction in this kind of occasion? I don't know, but this would have to do.

'She's alive? Where... How?'

'I can't give you any details like that. Not without her permission. Can I give her your details? Give her a chance to get in contact with you.'

Kendra nodded rapidly. 'You can't tell me anything more?'

'Not without clearance, or some sort of legal persuasion.'

'Christine, could you, do you know something?' Kendra looked at me as though I would be able to solve everything on the spot, but I had to disappoint her. It wasn't a situation anyone would have much experience with. I'd never come across it before.

'I'm sorry. I think that Erik's right. If we're talking about a fully competent adult,' I raised my eyebrows at him and he nodded, 'then we can't force the issue. It's like an adoption.'

'It's not like a fucking adoption!'

Kendra's vehemence was so sudden and so unlike her usual demeanour that it took me by surprise. I got over myself and started to put my hand towards her but she turned to me in anger.

'And don't stick your hand on me again. I don't need your bloody sympathy I need my bloody daughter.'

Erik raised his hands to try to offset some imaginary coming violence, but I ignored him as I pulled Kendra close, quite obviously against her wishes, and whispered in her ear.

'I know who it is.'

***

I knocked on the door while Kendra hung back, hugging herself, white-knuckled. She scanned the street in her best impression of someone yelling out "I shouldn't be here. I'm doing something wrong".

'Are you okay? Are you sure you want to do this?' I asked. I'd been asking since we got back in the car to come here and her frown showed she was getting sick of it, but I couldn't stop myself. I was finding it hard to process everything. I assume that Kendra was having even more trouble than I was.

Once I'd stood there for two minutes with no answer, I relaxed. She wasn't home. She wasn't home at the address I shouldn't know but had mysteriously come to me as I sat opposite Erik merrily reading upside down. I had to love him sometimes.

I knocked once more just to put on the appearance of not giving up that easily, but I was happy to find the tight knots were gradually unravelling in my stomach.

'Should we go?' I asked, and then heard the sound of movement inside.

Bugger.

I scanned the street and then looked back at the front door. Everything along the way was completely quiet. One or two houses had a definite slump to their frames, and there was an interesting property two doors down on the other side of the street which seemed to have a garage that had mysteriously been placed one whole foot above the house that conjoined it.

Not to mention the dried liquefaction that replaced the traditional front lawn on some of the houses.

We were in the red zone. No wonder she didn't want to come to the door. There was no way she was allowed to be here. The police would usually have made an effort to move on a squatter but I made the assumption that they either had other things on their mind, or were looking the other way considering the circumstances they'd come to this knowledge by.

'Sarah,' I called in a loud whisper right by the door. I looked around me again, and thought about why my mother had given birth to an idiot. There was no one around to hear me.

'Sarah, it's Christine Emmett. I met you before when I was helping out the Sutherlands. I'm not here to cause any trouble. Would you be able to let me in?'

'I turned down the offer of victim support,' came the muffled response. 'I don't need your help.'

'I just wanted to talk to you. I'm not here as support, I'm just here as a person.'

'There's someone with you.'

'Yes, this is my friend Kendra. She's a member of the same support group that I am.' I made the assumption that Erik would already have talked to her. 'Have you heard of her?'

'Kendra who?'

'Kendra Little,' Kendra said behind me, nudging me to one side as she came forward to be fully in view of the door's side windows.

'My name is Kendra Little. I'm your mother.'

There was a long silence from the other side of the door. Then Sarah started to shout. I could hear the tears in her voice as she did so.

'I don't have a mother. I told the officer I didn't want to see you. You're not allowed to do this. He told me you're not allowed.'

'Sarah, I'm sorry, you're right,' I said at the same time as Kendra chimed in.

'You do have a mother. She's standing outside. She's waiting to see the daughter that she's been missing every day for the last forty years and she's not going anywhere until you let her in.'

'I'm calling the police,' Sarah yelled back.

'Call them then, dear. I'm not going anywhere.'

There was a furious thumping on the door. I stepped back in a hurry. It sounded like she was throwing herself or something equivalently large to whack it with considerable force.

'You're not allowed. He said he couldn't pass on my name.'

'That's correct, dear,' Kendra yelled back through the door. 'Just like you can't live in a red-zone house. And yet here we both are.'

There was silence in response. And silence for a long time after. I grew tired of standing, and sat down on the dusty front step. The shadows lengthened and the stone which started out cold under my butt turned warm and then started to press my cheeks against my tailbone. I shifted from side to side to try to ease the pressure.

I jumped as there was a soft murmur from inside the house.

Kendra moved to the door and placed her ear up to the wood. 'What was that?'

There was silence again. For long minutes it dragged out. And then the murmur again, a bit louder.

'Dad told me that you didn't want me anymore. Dad told me that you'd given me to him at a pub one night because I was too much work.'

Kendra sank down to her knees. I thought at first it was with the weight of the revelation, but then realised that she was trying to adjust herself down to the matching position of her daughter inside, so she could quietly answer.

'But you know that's not true, don't you? You've known that for a while haven't you? It's what he would've told the others too.'

There was no response except silence again.

The setting sun caught the last glimmers of cloud on the horizon, and set a strange golden light over the suburb. It made everything around me look as though it were part of a seventies film.

Kendra had started tapping a small pattern on the surface of the door. It reminded me of the way Rena had tapped out patterns on the cover of her hospital bed.

'Do you want me to go and wait in the car?' I asked quietly. 'Give you two a bit of privacy.'

Kendra shook her head. 'That's okay. It's not like I have any secrets left. Not from you anyway.'

I smiled back at her from the step. It was weird being here in these circumstances. There was so much hope and opportunity; loss and regret. As though we were on the verge of something big that might change the course of everything. Or might just fizzle away into nothing.

Not that it would change things for me anyhow. It wasn't my daughter trapped behind the door. Refusing to see me.

'Do you want me to tell you a story, Sarah?' Kendra asked. Her voice was raised to be heard through the door, and there was a slight echo back from the empty houses in the deepening twilight.

'I used to have a little girl. She was special to me. She helped me to overcome a whole lot of things that I was doing that I shouldn't have been. That sounds really selfish, I know, but it was true.'

She shifted her weight so her back was against the door. She let her head fall back against it, and closed her eyes. Lost in memory.

'I loved her a whole lot more than I thought I would,' she laughed briefly. 'When I first found out I was pregnant I was so scared and freaked out. I didn't know who the father was. I didn't know much at all about anything I was doing at the time. It took me a while to even know I was pregnant, that's how out of it I was. I didn't really keep track of my periods or anything like that, and throwing up in the morning was something that I was already familiar with.'

She shifted again. Stretched her legs out fully and crossed them at the ankle. The heels of her feet hung out over the first step.

'I was really scared that when I gave birth there would be something wrong. By that stage I'd sobered up completely. My GP hadn't given me much to stay away from – not like these days – and they didn't have things in the news about foetal alcohol syndrome and stuff like they have now, but you know just by reading an aspirin label that stuff can harm children, and lots of things weren't recommended for pregnant women. I thought there was a good chance that I'd done something irreversible. I worried for the whole five months I had left of my pregnancy. I was so worried that I didn't want to check with anyone whether it might be true in case they told me it was.' Kendra looked pensive for a moment then added, 'and of course then they'd have started talking about how Aunty Betty knew someone who knew someone who knew how to take care of things, and I wanted my baby more than I'd ever wanted anything in my life.'

'I struggled through the labour. It was awful. I didn't have anyone with me either. They didn't assign midwives or anything, and I didn't have anyone I could go to and ask about that sort of stuff. It was just me and the nurse in and out and the doctor turning up at the very end. I was so glad to have that over and done with. I swore then that I'd never do that again, and I held true to that over the years.'

'And then they took my baby away. I didn't know what was happening, and the nurse wouldn't answer me. Just straightened my pillow and asked if I felt up to showering on my own. The doctor didn't come back, and I thought my baby was dead. Until you disappeared years later that had been the worst thing I'd ever experienced.'

'Apparently you'd had trouble breathing. They took you away and used a wee tube to suction out your lungs. Nowadays they'd do all that sort of thing in the same room, they'd bring in all the equipment, have it all ready. Once they'd got you breathing okay they thought they'd keep you under observation for a while and make sure you kept breathing. I don't think it occurred to any of them to let me know what was happening. I thought you were dead. That I'd taken something, swallowed something, drank something before I knew I was pregnant and it had killed you before you even had a chance to be born.'

Kendra stopped for a moment. She was weeping steady tears, and she wiped them from her face and blew her nose.

'What happened then?'

The thin voice came from the other side of the door. It was clear, even though it wasn't loud. I smiled and lifted myself up a few inches, bracing with my hands and wrists to give my butt a chance to get some feeling back in it.

'Dear I know you don't want to let me into your house, but I'm an old lady. This concrete's awful hard and it's starting to get cold. I promise you I won't lay a finger on you and you can ask me to leave any time you want, but could you please let me come inside and get comfortable?'

I heard movement and then the sound of the lock being turned. The door slowly opened just enough for a sliver of face to be visible.

Sarah Jones looked a million miles from the woman who had stood calmly to one side while the dive team searched an underwater graveyard and the Sutherlands waited for their daughter's corpse to be found. Her hair hung in lank clumps, all of their curl gone. Her face settled in deep wrinkles, and it looked as though she'd been lying on something that had stained the side of her face slightly blue. Her eyelids barely opened. There were deep scratches to the side of her face, caused by fingernails by the look, and without any other culprit in the frame I guessed at her own hand.

'You can come in. I don't want her in here though.'

I happily took the chance to wander back to the car and settle into a seat that wasn't made of concrete. I turned on the radio to keep me company, and leaned the seat back until I was reclining halfway to the floor.

Kendra stepped inside her daughter's house. The first barrier fought and won.

***

I was sitting next to Gary again. Again there was no response. I'd talked with his doctor, trying not to impose my own assumptions upon him, and he was happy to leave him untreated for a while longer.

If Gary had been my patient I would've started up shock therapy to bring him out of his internal state by now. Which might be why ethics committees exist.

Luckily I was still quite fond of the sound of my own voice.

'Kendra and Sarah are down at the station today. Sarah's going to give another statement. The last time she didn't tell the police anything, and they had nothing to charge her with so they let her go.'

I laughed. 'The usual charge of wasting police resources couldn't really be used since she saved them so much by coming forward to begin with.'

'Kendra looked so peaceful when I left her. It'll be rough, but I think she'll benefit from this so much.'

I tried to pretend that Gary's complete silence was rapt attention, but it wore thin. When my phone rang I answered it a tad too eagerly.

'Christine. Can you come down to the station please? I need some help.'

'Ilene, what's wrong.'

'I don't know. They told me that they've found my little boy's body. But then they started to ask me some questions. I need someone here to tell me what's going on.'

Oh God. Poor Ilene. In the excitement of finding out Kendra's child was alive I'd forgotten that Ilene was also awaiting results.

'I'll be there as soon as I can. Hold tight until then. If they try to ask you anything that upsets you, just tell them you're not going to say anything until I get there. Okay?'

When I came in through the door Ilene was sitting with an officer next to her. I felt a chill run through my body at the sight of that. They didn't trust her enough to leave her alone.

She stood and flew into my arms as soon as she saw me. Her body was shaking hard.

'What's happening,' I whispered straight into her ear, so that no one else would hear. 'What are they asking you?'

She just shook her head, and I heard nothing but the

fast puffs of her breath in return.

'Ma'am. Okay ma'am. Are you ready to assist us again?'

I turned to look at the man who now stood next to Ilene.

'And you are?' I asked. I tried to interject some note of haughtiness into my voice, but I was too shaken by Ilene's obvious distress to be successful.

'Sergeant Moorley, ma'am.'

'And what have you been asking my client that's led to her current level of distress?'

'She's been asked questions relating to the inquiry. Are you a lawyer, because your client hasn't told us she was asking for a lawyer?'

'No I'm not a lawyer.'

'Then I'll have to ask you to wait outside while we resume our interview.'

'No. I won't answer any more of your questions,' Ilene shouted. She had the same strident tone that she used when she went off on a rant about the evils of modern medicine.

What on earth was going on?

'Sergeant Moorley. Is there any chance that you could postpone this interview until tomorrow? It's obvious that Ms Mainard is upset at the moment, and I think she'd benefit from a rest before continuing.'

'Christine. What's going on here?'

I turned and was grateful to see Erik striding across the room.

'Hi Erik,' shit! Not the right time. 'I mean Detective Senior Sergeant Smith. My friend has been greatly distressed by an interview this morning, and I was merely asking if further questioning could be postponed until tomorrow.'

Erik raised his eyebrows at Sergeant Moorley, but whatever signals the two men were using they came back unfavourable to Ilene.

'No, that won't be possible. We can agree to let you and Ms Mainard have a break for the next half hour, but we need to continue with our line of questioning today.'

I opened my mouth to object, but he shook his head

firmly before I could get a word out.

'Ms Mainard is quite welcome to retain council if she needs to, but we won't postpone for anything else. If you don't want to take a break then we can resume questioning immediately.'

There were alarm bells ringing all over my head now, but I had no idea what was going on. How was I meant to defend my friend when I was in the dark?

'Is it okay if we sit in my office until then?'

'Just keep the door open.'

He walked away and started to talk with a woman over by the soft interview room. She was tall, and dressed well. Professional at something, but what I couldn't guess.

'Come on Ilene. It's through here.'

I led the way and pulled my chair around to the front of the desk so we could sit side by side. She sat down on the edge of the chair, but her gaze was firmly locked on Officer Moorley who remained in place. I moved my chair further around to break the view.

'Can you tell me what's going on?'

'I don't know. They called me to ask me to come in, and told me I could bring a lawyer if I needed to. Then they started to ask questions about Angie.'

I still wasn't following.

'You said that they told you they had a match with your test results?'

Ilene nodded. 'It took ages before they got around to telling me that. I think they wanted to make me break down or something. But then it was back to their stupid questions. How often did she spend time with Brian? Was she registered with a GP? How many times had I been to the emergency room with her?'

'Then they wanted to know about the custody hearings and the court case. Like I can remember all the details all this time later. They would ask me questions and I'd answer, and then they'd pull out some transcript or file and read out what my answer was nine years ago and how they didn't match and then they'd ask me to explain myself.'

I looked carefully at Ilene. I knew that she'd been

involved in a custody case at the time Brian and Angie had disappeared. Until the grisly discovery at the pond I think everyone had just followed the obvious thread that he'd taken her away rather than risk losing custody. But I didn't know about the emergency room visits.

'Was Angie in your custody at the time she disappeared?' I asked, my voice as gentle as I could manage.

'No, she was staying with Brian. He was awarded temporary full custody until a decision was made.'

Ilene had always had a thing about doctors. She'd always had a thing about medicine. I'd always assumed she had grown attached to alternative medicine – or non-medicine as I usually called it – as many people did.

But she was talking about GPs and emergency rooms. That wasn't where you took your child if you had a genuine distrust of effective western medicine. That was where you took your child when they were hurt, and you expected they could make your child well.

And if she had accepted it for her child, what made her reject it now.

I felt cold as I thought of all the questions that I'd never put to Ilene. It was natural to bond with someone over all the things you have in common. It was the currency of friendship. But it looked like there were answers here that I'd never dreamed of finding.

'Ilene. Did you ever hurt Angie?'

She turned a hurt expression onto me, but it melted away into pure anger.

'How dare you ask me that? You've known me for years. You must know that I'd never...' she fumbled for words to finish her sentence but although her mouth moved there was nothing there to fill it. She swallowed hard and looked at me with contempt. 'You're just like all the others.'

CHAPTER THIRTEEN

Sarah's Story

For most of my life it was just my Dad and me. He had a bit of a temper. He could become violent at the flick of a switch. I knew better than to ignite him though. I knew from experience.

I was always good. I always followed the rules. I was too timid to do anything else I think. Too scared of the consequences of doing wrong.

The first sibling I remember I think I was about four or five. No, not five. I wasn't in school yet. Four.

Melissa; she didn't last long. She was mouthy and loud. When she didn't have anything to say she'd scream instead. She made me cringe every time she did that. She made my skin pull tight as though it was trying to get behind something else rather than being the first point of contact for my body.

My Dad slapped her a few times. I got the point but Melissa didn't. One time he slapped her across the face and her head hit against the door really hard. There was a spatter of blood that sprayed out across the wallpaper and I had to carefully scrub it off later. Carefully because if I damaged the wallpaper Dad might get mad again. Maybe not that day but seeing it every time he walked by the spot he'd get angrier and angrier and then one day it would all be too much and he'd get mad again. At me. I didn't want him to get mad at me.

Melissa was quiet for a while after that hit. She had blood running down her face and it got in her eyes. It must have hurt. She rubbed it away and didn't say anything for the rest of the day.

It didn't last long though. The next morning she was mouthing off again. The morning after that she was screaming. The morning after that Dad pulled her by the arm so hard I could hear the pop of her shoulder. He took her outside. After a while I couldn't hear her scream anymore. I never saw her again.

I was excited the first day of school. That's what my Dad told me I was, and so that's what I was. If I had to explain what I was feeling that day it would have been naked fear. Stripped back wide-eyed fear. But Dad called it excitement and so did I.

There were kids there. They all seemed to know what to do. Where to go. When to line up. When to play. They knew each other's names and they knew the teacher's name. I didn't, and I didn't know how to know that.

It seems funny looking back, but it wasn't at the time. I didn't understand that you could learn something. That you could hear something and then remember it later. I thought they all just had this knowledge sitting there. They had it all sitting there and I had none of it. I had no idea what I was meant to do.

I got there in the end. I'm sure by the end of the first month in school I knew when to line up and when to play too. It just didn't feel like that to me. I always seemed to be two or three steps behind everyone else.

My Dad would pick me up from down the road. I would walk out of school and then cross the road and go down the street. There was a large tree there, and he'd be parked beside the tree. I would get in the car and we'd go home.

One day a teacher asked me if my father was picking me up after school. She made me sit down on the wooden three plank seats outside my classroom.

I tried to tell her that I was okay. My Dad was picking me up it was just down the road, but I was never very good at explaining myself to the authorities. Not at age five. Not now. My voice didn't work or my mouth didn't form the words or the words weren't in the right order. Whatever the reason my message didn't make it from my brain to their brain.

I picked at the dark green paint. I found after a while that I'd pulled up the edge of the hole. When I dragged it back further it would come off in a long strip.

I denuded almost a foot of the plank furthest from the summerhill stone wall while the teacher watched the road.

I don't know how long I sat there. My stomach pulsed and my throat started to throb with the tears of anger and frustration that I would not shed.

Dad pulled up opposite the school.

I didn't ask for permission. I stood up, grabbed my backpack, and started to run.

The teacher grabbed my shoulder, and I turned without thinking and kicked her in the shin. I ran to the car and got in the back seat. The tears that I'd held back for so long came tumbling out. I tried to cry without making a sound. Dad didn't like sound. My chest hitched and pulled with the effort.

I thought I would be in trouble at home, but Dad never even mentioned it. I thought I would be in trouble at school, but the teacher didn't ever talk to me.

I asked my Dad one day if I'd ever have a brother or a sister. A lot of the children in my class had them. They had a mother as well, but I thought that my Dad was enough parent for me. A sibling would be good though. At times I even thought back to Melissa and wondered if she would've been a sister if she'd stayed.

I didn't know much about how brothers and sisters arrived, but I had suspicions that it wasn't the way Nina arrived. Dad just pulled her out of the back seat of the car one weekend, and there she was. Fully formed. She was only a little smaller than I was. I may not have been exposed to much, but I had seen a baby before, and Nina certainly wasn't that.

Nina was quiet and suspicious. Her thumb stayed in her mouth most of the time, while her big brown eyes followed Dad and me whenever we moved. I heard Dad tell her once that her mother didn't want her anymore. That must have been hard for her to hear. She cried and cried; all without ever making a sound.

When Dad served up a meal I knew to eat it all. Not too fast because that was disgusting, but not too slow because that didn't show appreciation for the effort that had gone into making it.

Nina didn't know this. When I told her what to do she ignored me. She would pick at the food. Move it around with her fork and occasionally put a bite in her mouth.

She grew thin and pale. My Dad's face grew thin and pale.

He wasn't upset with her the same way that he would've been with me. He didn't yell and pull at her the same way he would've done with Melissa.

I think it was because she was so little. By this time I measured myself ¾ of the way to the door handle, but Nina was far shorter than that. And not just short. She was thinner as well. She also had the most amazing straight dark brown hair. I envied it so much over my own pale curls.

Dad may not have been angry with Nina, but every day she grew thinner he grew angrier with me.

I too tried to become smaller and quieter, but he still saw me there. I still annoyed him. One time he picked me up and threw me down flat on the floor. I was winded and I banged my head so hard that lights shone steady and bright in my eyes, even when they were closed.

Having a little sister wasn't all that I'd imagined it to be. I no longer remembered why I'd wanted one.

Nina looked at me with big sad eyes across the dinner table one night just before she pitched forward onto her plate. I didn't know what to do. Should I keep eating until my plate was empty, or was there another *rule that I should follow?*

Dad picked Nina up and put her to bed. I cleaned up her plate by knifing the scraps into the rubbish bin. I washed it under the tap and dried it off with the tea towel and put it away. I then finished eating my tea for good measure.

Dad didn't come back into the dining room. I put myself to bed when it was time. I tried to be quiet.

Dad checked in my room before he went to bed. I held myself rigid and still. He may be angry. I may have earned myself a punishment. He kissed me on the forehead then went to bed.

I went into Nina's room the next day. I wanted to check and see if she was okay. She was quiet as usual. She was lying flat on the bed her eyes closed.

I crept close and placed a kiss on her forehead just as Dad had on mine the night before.

Her skin was cold, her eyelids were blue, she stank.

By the time I got home from school that day she was also gone.

Dad was angry for a long time after Nina. Sometimes when he got drunk at night and looked at me over the rim of his whisky glass I thought that he wished I were dead. He hit me a lot more, beat me a lot more, hurt me a lot more after Nina.

I learned to stay out of his way though. I worked hard at making him happy, and eventually he came out of his withdrawal and went back to being my Dad again.

I no longer wanted a brother or a sister.

There were others over the years as I grew up. I tried to keep myself separate. Sometimes they learnt the rules and they would stay a while. Others were gone within days.

Dad would turn up battered and bruised. Once his shoulder was pushed well out of its socket. He made me hold onto it while he twisted his body back together. It hurt him incredibly to do so. I knew this because he socked me in the side of the head when it finally settled back into place.

I learned how to cook for Dad. I learned how to

clean up after the two of us, or the three of us.

I learned how to do laundry and vacuum and clean up blood from the different surfaces throughout our home. Sometimes mine; sometimes not.

At school sometimes I would fall asleep in the playground, lying in the sun. Once, there was talk of bringing in my father to talk it all over, and I learned not to do that again.

The other kids at school grew into teenagers. They talked about music and about cars and about clothing and about movies. I stayed quiet and listened but I didn't know what they were talking about. We didn't have the things that they did at home. Dad would never allow it.

They changed their hair and started to wear make-up. They looked forward to mufti days when they could display their fashion knowledge, and they talked about what they'd wear to the senior's dance for years prior to the event.

I didn't go to the dance.

They talked about work and Polytech and University and their big OE.

I started to wonder about that myself.

Even though I didn't concentrate much at school I'd also had good marks. The teachers thought I was bright even though I "didn't apply myself." One day Mr Jefferson pulled me aside and told me that I was natural in science and was I seriously considering university because if I was he could line me up with some scholarships to take care of my living expenses while I attended.

The idea took hold in my mind. I'd never had a dream for myself before and I took care of it. I'd only pull it out and examine it when Dad was asleep or away. I'd pull it out and look at it and think about what it would mean.

The time to make a decision came and I didn't even know how to approach it with Dad. I struck my old problem of not knowing how to talk to someone in authority. I didn't know how to phrase it or how to convey what I wanted. I didn't know how he would *react or what he would think or if he would let me go.*

I put it off and put it off until the time was almost up.

And then he brought home Allie.

She was different from the others. She quickly learned how to keep her mouth shut unless she was offering praise. She quickly learned the rules on how to dress and when to speak and how to eat.

When Dad told her that her parent's didn't want her anymore she didn't cry. When he told her she should be grateful that he was looking out for her she just nodded her head and said thank you.

He talked about enrolling her in school the next year. He talked about how she was a fine little sister to have and that he cared for her very much. I could hear him at night showing her how much, and I was glad that she was there and I might finally be allowed to be free.

I broached the subject one night when Dad had woken me up to sit up with him and listen to the radio.

I sat next to him with his hand on my knee and listened to old ladies complain about the council and how they weren't doing anything to stop the people parking on the lawn.

I told him there was a wonderful opportunity to earn a scholarship and go to university and how it would bring money into the household. I told him that if I studied hard and passed then I would be able to attend and I could pass the money onto him. I told him that Allie was already learning how to cook and clean and she would easily be able to help him out and I would come home after every lecture just as I came home straight after school and there wouldn't be any difference except that I would be able to learn and earn a degree and then when I went out to work I'd be able to get more money and everything would work out and be great forever.

When I woke up it was dark and every part of body either ached or throbbed. When I tried to move the pain grew worse and I didn't seem to be able to get very far. There was no light, no light that I could see at all. I began to think that I was blind. I began to think that I was trapped. I began to scream in pain and fear and anguish.

I don't know how long I was like that. Long enough that I stopped screaming in pain because the pain wasn't as bad as the hunger. Long enough that I stopped worrying about the hunger because the hunger wasn't as bad as the thirst. Long enough for my tongue to sit as a swollen dry thing in my mouth and for each minute I slept there was water, glorious water, everywhere but always just out of reach.

When the sounds of freedom came I thought they were the sounds of my death. Although I felt fear I also felt calm that it would finally be the release from all the torment.

Instead of release there was a straw and sips of water. Instead of release there was a forkful of food, a pulling of my body back into the light which burned my eyes even when I closed them against it.

He never buried me down in the coffin again. He didn't have to. From that day forward I carried it with me.

CHAPTER FOURTEEN

Screaming. At first I bolted to the door in the expectation people would start to evacuate, but there were just startled looks. Out of my office I could hear the sound more clearly and the resemblance to a siren diminished. I moved closer to the sound just as Erik pushed open the door of the soft interview room.

'Christine,' he said. His usual authority was shaken and my name sounded more like a plea. 'I don't know what to do.'

I hurried the rest of the distance. The scream had lowered in volume, but apart from a short break to take in air and start anew, it showed no other sign of stopping.

Sarah was perched on the edge of the couch, her knees pulled up towards her stomach. Her arms crossed in a tight hug of such strength I could see the clear knot of muscle in her shoulders.

'What,' Erik began, but I motioned for him to go outside, and closed the door.

I didn't worry about talking - she was well beyond that stage. I added my own arms on top of Sarah's self-hug and pulled her rigid body to me.

The scream continued, lower again. There was another short intake of breath and the hard lines of her body jerked once; an attempt to shake me free. I didn't release her, and she didn't try again. Her body also didn't soften.

I tried to pull her back towards me, and then roll her forward to start a swaying motion to try to ease her tension. Sarah held tight in her locked position though, and I settled for rocking my own body back and forth, extending and contracting my arms to keep her body in close contact.

When I'd been in Thailand years ago, a local masseuse had told me one night about her theory on how the body retained bad emotional experiences in its muscles.

'In situations where you have a sudden shock, like if you hear a sudden noise, your body fills up with adrenalin, right?' she'd said. It was close enough to the truth that I'd nodded in response.

'So usually what happens is that you run away, or you work out that it was just a car backfiring, and your brain sends out some more wee chemical messengers that tell your cells the crises is over and they let all that adrenalin just flow on back out.'

My drunken retort had been lost on her, and she'd continued, 'but when your body doesn't know what's happened, right? When the brain doesn't send the message to release all those nasty chemicals back out of your body your cells lock up like this.' She'd clenched her hand tight into a fist. 'And the cell basically dies, right? But years later when they're on my massage table and I'm getting deep into their tissue I come across these cells, and they start to relax and release their chemicals. They start to wake up again, but when they do all those bad memories of all the shit that was happening when they died, right. It all comes back out too. And I have to tell them it's okay, everything's going to be okay, and after a while they can tell me what went wrong and just let the whole bad memory go.'

It had been a ridiculous conversation. I don't know if Gary and I had laughed about it afterwards, but it was the sort of thing we would have done. Laughed at the foolish notion of the hippies that plagued the area.

Holding Sarah in my arms, and rocking my body back and forth however, I felt her start to soften. I could see in my mind's eye her cells, her long-dead cells filled with chemicals, open up and start to release their toxins back out into the world.

As her volume grew ever lower, and my rocking motion began to transfer its energy to a sway in Sarah's body, I envisioned the cells opening up to let every bad memory they held within flow back out.

Ten minutes passed while we rocked back and forth, and she relaxed further and further into my hug.

'I've wet myself,' she said at last, with a soft child-like voice full of shame.

'It doesn't matter,' I replied, and let my arms fall back so they no longer encircled her fully. 'There's a shower right through there,' I nodded my head at the adjoining room. 'There's towels and I'll ask them to get your some clean clothes.'

'I can't do it,' she stated.

'It's okay,' I replied, 'I'll wait right outside,' but her head moved back and forth in denial of my words.

'I can't do it.'

She started to stand, and then sat again with her cheeks flushed. The sharp tang of her urine hung in the air.

'I'll get you a towel,' I said and moved to the door. I could leave the room for a minute so she'd be able to move into the adjoining en-suite without me watching.

'I don't need a towel. I need that man to leave me alone.'

I frowned. 'You mean Detective Smith?'

'I'm not going back there.'

I moved a step towards her, but Sarah pressed back into the couch.

'I'll get you a towel, and some clean clothes. Let's start there.'

If she replied I didn't know. I walked straight out of the room and closed the door.

'Has she calmed down?'

I nodded, but when he tried to move past me to the room I held up my hand.

'She needs some clean clothes.'

He looked me up and down, and then jerked his head at officer Walker who immediately walked off in obedience.

'She can have a shower and clean herself up, but make sure she's as quick as possible. We need to get moving.'

'What do you mean?' I asked. Then worked out the answer before he needing to speak. 'Erik, I don't think that's a good idea today. Sarah's scared out of her mind. She's in no condition to go anywhere.'

'We need to find Chloe. We can't afford to wait any longer. She should've told us all of this from the beginning.'

I didn't know what she'd told him, but I could still feel the hard rock of tension that'd been Sarah's body just a few minutes earlier.

'No one's stopping you going,' I said. 'But you can't take her anywhere. She's in no fit state.'

'She can't tell us where it is. She doesn't know the direction of anything, or the distance to anywhere, or even the name of a road, or a street, or a lane. Ms Jones is the only way we're going to find our way anywhere, and we need to do that now. Today.'

I can't do it. I'm not going back there.

'Come on, Christine. You know I'm right. We can't leave a four year old girl out there to die just because she's had a rough time. You know this.'

Of course I knew it.

'I'm coming with you then. And you'll need to call in the station doctor so we can get her some anxiety relief. I'm not going to let her be traumatised any more than I have to.'

Erik strode past me without acknowledgement, but I trusted that he'd heard.

I turned and went back into the soft interview room. Back to try to explain to someone that yes they were going to do the one thing they couldn't do.

***

The injection given to Sarah turned her eyes glassy, and her muscles to play dough. Completely pliable, I'd helped her into the back of the unmarked vehicle. After a few minutes on the road her head rolled to one side, but she snapped it back upright again. Fighting back against the drug.

She issued occasional instructions, and once I had to help her lean forward to have a close look at an intersection before she decided on the route and leant back.

The flow of other traffic thinned and then ceased as we began to take roads that changed from two-lane blacktop to single lane, no markings, to shingle, to dirt.

Large tree branches criss-crossed over the top of the road we travelled at lower and lower speeds, a cloud of dust in our wake. There was a final turn and the road stopped. Even at our reduced speed the brakes were slammed on and Sarah fell forward, her head banging on her knees.

'Where now?' Erik asked as I tried to see if there was any other way through.

Sarah's glassy eyes scanned the view from her window. She jerked her head back the way we'd come. 'Back there. There's a turn-off.'

Erik's fingers clenched on either side of the steering column. The set of his shoulders was stiff. I couldn't remember seeing a turn-off either, but he started the vehicle up and reversed it, and turned it back.

I saw it almost at once, as did Erik. The turn-off was angled sharply back, hiding it from casual glances when heading the other way. Leaves covered the entrance, it should look unused. Instead I had an image of a man manually spreading them across the width of the lane, a careful disguise.

Erik slowed the car even more as we made the turn and advanced along the thin track. A cloud floated in front of the sun and the drive immediately faded to dusk.

'I can't,' Sarah whispered next to me. Her hair hung in a curtain over her face so I couldn't tell for sure, but I thought she was crying. She gave a low groan and the hairs on the back of my neck raised. I put my arm around her shoulders but she let herself fall forward away from my embrace. Bent in half she tucked her hands under her legs and pressed her face against her legs.

'I'll stay with you Sarah. You're not alone. I won't let anything bad happen to you.' The words felt empty in the face of her turmoil.

'It's around the next turn,' she whispered.

Erik pulled the car to a stop. He looked in his rear-view mirror to see that the other vehicles did the same, then got out of the car. 'Stay there,' he said as he walked back to the next vehicle.

Sarah kept her head down on her knees. I moved my own head down to brush the hair back from her face and look at her. 'Thank you so much for doing this Sarah. It means a lot to Chloe's parents.'

The only response was a shake of her head.

I heard the roar of a car engine. I started to raise my head up, but a heavy crunch of metal the whole car was moving, pushed back. A roar, a screech, and Sarah slammed into me. I fell backwards but didn't move from my seat. Sarah shrieked in pain. Her weight was on me. I saw her leg caught in a twist of leather and metal that had been the seat, or the door, or the boot.

Shouts and the sound of motion outside, but then another push of force. My head collided with hard plastic. I saw black, and white, and black, and stars.

***

Sarah's Story

The earthquake was when everything really changed for me.

For years, I put up with it all. I watched my father drag his disgusting body around the house. I watched him mess up everything that I tidied, and smell up everything I aired out, but I put up with it. There wasn't another choice. Not for me. Just accept the crap that is your life and try to get by. That's all some of us deserve.

And then one morning I was jolted out of bed.

I scrabbled on the floor like a rat. It was hard to get my feet under me, but the white hot signal flashed in my brain – get to a doorway. Stand in the doorway. You're going to die if you don't get to a doorway.

My primary school teachers scornful face in my head. Her instructions in my ear.

I crawled on my belly in the end.

When I reached the door frame I pushed myself up to my feet again, and slammed my back into the frame, with my arms braced against the other side.

There was a thunder. A noise that sounded everywhere and nowhere all at once. I thought the ground was quieting down, I started to relax, and then the worst of it came. The ground bucked back and forth, and my hair swung in time with the open cupboards; with the falling glassware.

The knowledge that I was about to die was absolute.

I was going to die in this shitty hole. My entire life used up. I hadn't achieved a single thing. I'd never done anything outside of school and the constraint of these four walls. These four foul walls.

I howled with a fury so intense that I thought it would burn me before the roof had a chance to cave in and claim me.

This shitty hole had stolen my life.

It had been so long since I'd felt an emotion apart from faint disgust, that it took me a moment to realise when the earthquake stopped.

My body was energised with fear and fury.

For the first time in decades my old dream came back to me full-force.

I had to get out.

Allie was long dead now. Got on the wrong side once too often. I'd had to help him drag the body to his "cemetery" – he'd been too ill or too hungover to cope alone – and as I helped him weight the body and sink it down I felt a pang of envy that I couldn't drift down beside it to lie still in the quiet of the lake; untroubled.

Dad had brought home a tiny baby a year or two ago. Who knew how long? There was no marker to the days or the weeks or the months when your life was grey drudge. The baby was walking now though, so a year at least.

I thought that I enjoyed the baby. I thought that when she smiled at me I felt happy. That when she touched and pulled my lips down with her tiny little fingers with their tiny little fingernails I felt joy.

My newfound fury taught me that I was wrong.

It turned out that I only loved that she would set me free.

He was distracted by her more as she grew older. I could see his foul interest pique and twist and grow to match.

The need to protect her was a pull deep in my belly.

The fury was an engulfing hunger. It won.

I spent time building up a small stash of money. With each aftershock I felt the fury growl, and the fear would leap on my shoulder and shout 'Late. You're too late. You're too old. You're too stupid.'

But it turned out I wasn't.

One day as he lay in a stinking heap on the stained bed-sheets, alcohol miring him in unconsciousness, I lay the baby down next to him.

Just put her down and walked out the door.

I managed to find a way through the afternoon and evening and night and I made a long journey into a city I'd never seen before at a time I'd never been out before.

I found a motel. It announced that it was low price but it still took more money than I had expected. I needed to find a new place to live, but I didn't know how.

I found an abandoned house in a street that had been affected by the earthquake. As long as I was careful about where I was in the house during the day, I could go undetected. Without the need to pay daily room rates my money stopped leaking away and I could relax and start thinking of what I could do next.

I found a cash job cleaning motel rooms. It was a job I knew well and once I'd shown how hard I could work over a few days the owner was happy to guarantee me hours each week.

The other room cleaners were mostly foreign. They found this city as funny and strange to live in as I did, and I started to make a few friends.

I tried hard not to think of my old life. It was easy to do that during the day. I concentrated on my work, and budgeting out my next week, and what I could afford for a treat if I felt like it. I kept my history to myself. I knew how the world treated a slut.

At night I sometimes stared at the ceiling with my eyes open, too scared to close them and see straight into my memory. When the lack of sleep showed I was given tips and tricks by my new friends, but these were images that thinking of sheep wasn't going to cure.

Sometimes I saw the baby I'd left behind. Sometimes I missed her. Sometimes I gave her thanks. Mostly I tried not to think of her. I knew too well what she had in store. Dwelling on it would be no help.

And now I think of all the things I could've done which would've helped her.

The longer I stayed away the further behind the memory was, but the stronger my ability to help that baby girl, and the greater the betrayal when I didn't.

Hindsight is hard.

There were more earthquakes. More upheaval. An earthquake which ruined a day's shopping, an earthquake which ruined a city centre and collected a body count, and an earthquake predicted by a moon man that didn't exist at all.

They meant ruin for others in the city. They meant a steady choice of housing for me. I could move closer to my work, and my motel work grew busier as the safe housing grew scant. I was taken on in a full time capacity and put on the books officially. I was paid more, and able to fit in more with those I met on a daily basis. I started to grow a true life.

And then one morning I saw an article on a website.

It was about a little girl that had gone missing. I shook my head at first. Of course I was making things up. Not every missing child in the world could be laid at his door. But then there was another article, scathing. It made it sound like the father had arranged for her to be kidnapped. It made it sound like he'd paid someone to do it. It made it sound like Dad. It made me think that the baby I'd left him with was dead.

I could've wept at the thought, but tears were cheap and dried easily. I'd thought I had come to terms with guilt, but that had been nothing in comparison to what I felt that morning.

There was only one way to see if it was deserved. I contacted the girl's parents and told them I knew where she was. I escorted them out to a place I'd hoped never to see again, and waited while they searched for a body, and when they found one I fervently hoped it was going to be somebody else's darling.

But it wasn't.

When the image of the toddler's body flashed across the screen I recognised her immediately. She lay on her side in the muddy stinking water, and the guilt lay firmly at my door.

I should've told them. I could've told them. When the guilt piled at my door. But then that officer told me I had to tell the truth, I had no choice, and I felt my fury bite back. I had a choice. It was the only thing I'd ever managed to give myself. A choice.

***

'Christine. Christine can you hear me?'

I nodded and the movement caused so much pain that I cried out.

'Christine.'

'I can hear you,' I shouted back. 'I'm stuck. Or something.'

I couldn't move my head for the pain. There was slick, sticky blood on my legs. It felt as though I was being hugged hard by padded steel piping. I couldn't see more than light and dark, moving shadows.

'The fire service is here. They're going to try to cut you out now.'

I tried to move again, and felt nothing but hard surfaces. I flexed my hand. I couldn't feel the soft warmth of skin. Bile rose in my throat.

'Sarah! Where's Sarah?'

'She's out. Just hold still. We don't want you to try to move until we say okay?'

I followed their instructions while horrendous noises emanated from their equipment. The minutes dragged into an hour, and then another. And finally I was free.

A large fire officer tried to encourage me into a neck brace as soon as he was able to manoeuvre my head, but I resisted. When I was able to stand and move, I stumbled away from him.

Sarah was sitting on the side of the road. There was a paramedic seated nearby, but she was ignoring him and looking out at the road.

There was little left of the car that I'd been trapped in. Some had been cut away. Some had been crushed together like a used beer can. A ute with its front end bashed in sat to one side.

'What happened?' I asked. 'Did that hit us?'

Erik cocked his head to one side. 'He ran into you. Tried a couple of times. I could've told him he was wasting his time.'

'He, who?'

A nod to Sarah. 'The nutter that took her. That probably took Chloe.' He looked further up the road, and ran his hand through his hair. 'He's named Donald King, but I'm sure the media will have renamed him by the time we get home. Just a moment.'

He walked off to talk to the fire office and the paramedic. There was a few hands waved but they appeared to reach some sort of agreement. The fire service left, taking the jaws of life with them, but the paramedics honed in on me and Sarah. I guess we were on our way.

Just before I got into the vehicle I called out, 'What do you mean probably took Chloe? She hasn't been found?'

Erik shook his head. 'I've got a team searching this place. They've found nothing in the house or immediate grounds. We're waiting for a dog team.'

'What are you doing out here with us then?'

He glared at me for a moment. 'I was making sure you were both okay, alright? No need to thank me. God.'

He stalked away, not even acknowledging when I called after him, 'Thank you Erik.'

***

'Can I ask you something?'

The question took me by surprise. I'd been lying in bed waiting. I needed a chest x-ray to come back clean before I was allowed to be discharged, and it seemed that no one was available to read it just yet. Sarah had taken the chair next to my bed after her own discharge, but she hadn't said a word till now.

I shrugged and nodded. 'Sure.'

'How did you know, that day at the pond?'

I waited for more, but when it didn't come I prompted, 'know what?'

'You knew that I was just making stuff up. You told that officer I wasn't psychic. How did you know that?'

'I don't believe in psychics.'

Sarah grimaced and frowned. 'I don't mean like that. I mean...' She slid further down in her chair, and kicked at the edge of the bed.

'I mean no one really believed that, did they? No one really thought I was communing with the dead or whatever. Not really, deep down. But they still weren't sure. When everything started to turn out the way I predicted.' She smiled, as though thinking of something pleasant. 'They almost thought I could be. And then you just glared at me, and walked off, and the next thing I know that cop arrested me. Off what you said.'

I nodded. It was a fair account.

'So why did you know? All of a sudden you seemed to know.'

I shrugged and looked out the end of the cubicle. The drawn curtains on either side blocked any view except straight ahead. 'It was what you'd said to me.'

'About what?'

'My daughter drowning.'

A frown appeared on her face, and then deepened as she looked down. 'But that was true wasn't it? I didn't make that up. I got your name off that conference with Rena. I googled you.' She looked up at me again, 'Anyway, I'd talked about that earlier. When you were with Rena. You looked terrified.' That smile again.

She'd googled me. Of course I knew that was how she'd known. It was obvious she hadn't been telling the truth. I ignored the tiny shred of disappointment. I can't give that shit room to grow.

'You got too many things wrong the second time, that's all. There was just other stuff going on and I knew that you weren't telling the truth.'

'What other stuff.'

'I...' I faltered and the sentence stopped before it'd really begun. 'There was just other stuff. Anyway, you knew you weren't psychic, why does it matter why I knew?'

Sarah wrapped her arms around herself, and I realised that my voice had come out louder than I'd meant it to.

'Sorry, I didn't mean to yell. It was just obvious to me, that's all. I can't really pinpoint why.'

She nodded and sat back, but with a pout on her lips. Whatever. I wasn't telling her anything about my little girl. She was my daughter, and that was my story.

They discharged me soon after. I caught a taxi with Sarah back to the station where I'd left my car a lifetime ago. I went to my desk to pick up my bag and keys and hoped I wouldn't see anybody I knew.

'Christine,' damn, 'How are you feeling?'

Allie pulled me into a hug that I winced my way out of.

'Nothing that won't heal. What are you doing here? I thought you'd be out at the crime scene.'

'Erik sent me home. They still haven't found Chloe. The dogs picked up her scent but just inside the house and they've gone over it with a fine-tooth comb. They're going to have a go at questioning Donald King next and see if they can get anything out of him.'

She clapped a hand over her mouth, then pulled it away and laughed. 'None of which I should be telling you.'

I felt a chill settle over my body. Poor Rena. Poor Ash. I should go to them.

'Christine?'

I turned to see Sarah who was still hanging around. I realised she mightn't have a way home. Maybe I should call Kendra?

'What is it?'

She pulled at my arm, and Allie took the hint and walked away while I backtracked to my office with Sarah. 'What is it?' I repeated when we were inside.

'Could you take me back out?'

'Sarah, if you have something that could help the police I'm happy to phone them for you, but I really don't think either of us are in any condition to go anywhere.'

She rocked up onto the balls of her feet. 'I can help. I can find her. But I can't do it over the phone. I don't know directions or distances or anything.' She paused and must have seen something in my face, something tired. 'It won't take long once we're out there. Please. If she's where I think she is we need to get to her now.'

And of course there was never any chance of saying no.

I signalled Allie to tell her our plan, and as hoped she offered to drive us out there. She also phoned ahead to let them know we were on our way.

It was full dark by the time we got there. Halogens had been strung up across the front of the house to try to illuminate the wider area, but it was hard to penetrate the woods that crept in all around. Allie pulled the car close in by the house and cut the engine. I looked at Sarah, her face was waxy pale in the fake sunlight.

'Didn't think I'd be seeing you again so soon, Ms Jones,' Erik called in greeting as he met us by the front door. 'Any assistance you can give us would be most welcome.'

Erik's height seemed to be disappearing under the weight of his tiredness. But as he swept his hand toward the house in welcome, he still managed a smile. 'There's stepping stones set down through the house. Try to keep to them otherwise forensics'll go mad.'

'Should we...' I was about to ask about covering, but he was already shaking his head, no.

Sarah looked back at me, and her face was slick with sweat despite the cool of the night. I stepped closer to her and touched her – fairy light – on her upper arm. She turned back and led the way into the house.

Into, and then through into the back yard. It was a small clearing and the only feature was an outhouse that smelled as if it still had frequent use. Sarah headed straight towards it.

She pulled away some dry branches that were piled to one side of the building, and knelt down in the bare space that was left. Erik moved forward with a large torch to shine light in the area.

There was a rope pull that lay almost flush with the dirt. I didn't understand. Sarah had stated she couldn't direct officers over the phone. She didn't know direction. This was the only other structure in the area – what direction did she think was needed?

She tugged and stepped back and up. A square of dirt lifted up from the ground. It was wood. The underside made that clear, but disguised on the top.

Erik moved further forward, his light held high. Sarah motioned him back and walked down into the hole in the ground she'd uncovered. He followed.

Allie stood back, but I wanted to see. I felt nervous. There was something wrong here. Something off. But I couldn't say what.

I knelt to the side and looked down into a room built underground. A cellar, except there was no house to top it. A dungeon.

I forced myself down the steps. In slow pursuit of Sarah and Erik. His light illuminated the main space belowground, but the shadows pressed in from the corners. Making the space smaller. Squeezing its dimensions.

Sarah's heels made a ridiculous tap on the heavy floor padded underneath with soil. She bent in a corner. I couldn't see. Even when Erik lifted the torch higher above her head I couldn't see.

I stumbled down the remaining steps feeling fear with the beat in my chest. Claustrophobia took my breath. I pushed myself forward, close behind Erik.

Sarah grabbed for something in the darkness. She raised it above her head and brought it crashing down. There was the thump of contact, the splintering of wood, and then a small cry. Sarah raised her arms above her head and brought them down. Up. Down.

Erik grabbed her and pulled her back. Pulled her away.

As she fell at my feet I saw the large mallet she'd held bounce out of reach. Sarah gave a roar of fury and scrambled after it. Erik kicked back at her as he knelt down next to a break in the floorboards. He dropped the torch to the floor as he shoved his hands underneath a shattered plank and forced up a lid.

My eyes tried to show me a fruit crate, but my mind showed me a coffin.

Erik pushed aside the lock that Sarah had hammered from the lid. He used shoulder to wedge up the opening. He reached his hands in and lifted out a draggled bundle. A draggled bundle that gave another faint cry.

My chest loosened enough to heave in a breath of air. A breath of stench.

Erik pushed past me, and ran up the stairs. Fleet as a dancer.

Sarah pushed to her knees and grabbed for the mallet. She raised her arms above her head and brought it down full force on the emptied box in front of her. In the fallen torchlight she looked like the villain out of a hundred horror movies. Mallet heaved up. Smashed down. Up. Down.

And she threw back her head as she gave a howl of anguish.

A scream of triumph.

***

Sarah's Story

And now there's a woman claiming to be my mother. My mother. What a joke.

What's the one fucking point to being a mother? The one defining characteristic? The one thing you're meant to do above everything else? Would it be to keep your child safe? Bingo.

Missed out on the big tick there, didn't you mother?

I told the police I didn't want to meet her. She was useless to me when I needed her. I wasn't about to spend time making her feel better about herself now that I didn't. Couldn't face her patting herself on the back because it all turned out okay, didn't it?

And then she turned up anyway. Turned up and wouldn't go away. She started to rave on about this and that outside my door, making all her apologies, making me sick. Telling me all her useless stories as though they were going to erase my past and make it all alright. All okay.

And yeah, I let her in. Yeah, I listened to her talk and I maybe let myself cry.

She was nice, after all. Nice to listen to, nice to hold. Nice to reassure me that everything was her fault.

Not quite so nice that the black stain on my soul faded away, not good enough for that, but not that far off. I found it hard to think about sending her away.

It's odd to see your smile in someone else's face. Odd to see the curve of your mouth abused by age. Odd to see that the thing you thought was a habit, turned out to be a mannerism. Turned out to be genetic.

I thought seriously for a moment of giving into her care. Of telling her my story and letting her try to heal me. She was asking for it. Offering it up as her one remaining service to me. There was a moment there when I could almost have done it. A moment when my mouth opened and if she hadn't chosen that exact second to speak maybe I would have let it out. A moment that passed.

And then I sank back into hating her. Like it was a

warm bath.

I've agreed to go to the station with her. I've agreed that I'll tell them where to find my Dad. I've agreed to try to help them find that little girl he's probably ruined by now.

I agreed because I think it'll be funny to see my mother's face as the police lay out one horror after another. As they detail every last little thing that her carelessness exposed me to. I agreed so I can watch her trying to pretend that everything could still be alright.

You want a burden, mother?

Strap yourself in.

CHAPTER FIFTEEN

Monday 18th November
Donald King death in custody
<u>The Christchurch Cradle Snatcher in Apparent Suicide</u>
<u>Officers waited 2 minutes before responding</u>

Two prison guards chose to "err on the side of caution" and wait for more than two minutes for help to arrive before entering Donald King's cell after the prisoner strangled himself.

King, commonly known as the Christchurch Cradle-Snatcher, died in Auckland maximum security prison Paremoremo a day before he was due to enter a plea charges relating to the serial killings of eight children and three adults in the years between 1974 and 2013. Further charges were pending in relation to the kidnapping and subsequent imprisonment of a woman over the same period.

At a press conference held late yesterday, police informed the press that King appeared to have strangled himself on Sunday with a piece of anti-suicide bedding located in the at-risk cell that he was transferred to after a routine risk-assessment highlighted him as an extreme suicide risk after he was remanded to Rolleston prison on his arrest.

King had already reacted violently on several occasions

during his incarceration, and was therefore classified as a "maximum safety" prisoner. This classification involved a strict protocol be followed when handling King, including the criteria that at least four guards be present in his cell when a response was required.

An internal investigation into the incident was announced by the Corrections Department. It has come to light that after the discovery that King had obscured security cameras into his cell and guards could see that his body was prone in the cell, they waited for over two minutes before entering the cell for extra guards to arrive in order to meet the protocol of his safety classification.

The prison spokesperson, Michael Macklan, who spoke on behalf of the guards actions yesterday has indicated that the guards were trained to "err on the side of caution" in all situations when dealing with violent prisoners. Although there were signs that King may be in trouble, it was also frequent that prisoners "faked" injuries such as falling over or laying prone in their cells, and could use resulting lapses in protocol to seriously injure corrections officers who attended to them.

'We have found no fault in the handling of this situation,' Macklan continued. 'We put strict protocols in place for a reason, and only adhere to them when it has been clearly demonstrated that a prisoner has a tendency to react in a violent manner. We stand by the actions taken by our staff on this occasion. Although it is always a grave situation when a prisoner comes to harm whether through the acts of others or themselves, we must also think of the safety and security of the officers who work in our prisons every day, and minimise the risk to them of harm in their workplace.'

It is not yet known whether Donald King was in restraints at the time of the incident.

The matter will be referred to the Coroner, and the results from the Corrections Department Inquiry will be made available to the public when the report is completed. This is expected to take place by the end of January.

CHAPTER SIXTEEN

Christine's Story

I spent years qualifying to become a psychiatrist; medical school, residency, specialisation. And then one day I was administering a drug to an emergency patient who, even if we could successfully acclimate them to a drug schedule would never be able to live an unassisted life, and I couldn't do it anymore.

As a psychiatrist you don't treat people in order to cure them and send them on their merry way. That's just a Christmas card. You drug them so they no longer pose a threat to themselves or others, often at the expense of any chance they have to live any sort of life. A cure? In psychiatry it's so rare that it's not even the focus any longer. My dreams of talking with patients and putting them on sophisticated regimens that would clear their brains so they could start to live in the real world evaporated in one instance, and I couldn't ever see a way clear to that coming back.

I tried to change the focus of my work. I changed my job so that I wasn't trapped in what was basically an asylum, no matter the politically correct names. I hung out my shingle in private practice, but it was even more forlorn than my previous role. I worked for the courts for a time, working as a specialist witness, and acting in consultation with the police and the prosecutors, but that just made me feel like a gun for hire. I couldn't have faith that my opinion was still without bias, so I couldn't continue.

It was just as I made the decision to leave that I found out I was pregnant. The timing was fortunate. And it gave me an excuse when I told Gary I'd decided to pack in my lucrative and long-fought for career.

To tell the truth, until my stick blossomed into a large blue cross, I'd started to think that pregnancy was something that wouldn't happen for us. For Gary and me. I'd started to think that we'd be one of "those couples" who had put their career in front of their family until it was too late. Not that I was too old to begin having a family. Just that sometimes not very old is still a bit late to have begun trying.

I changed my job from active treatment of patients, to paperwork on existing cases. The administration work was something that would've filled me with horror when I was studying, but now seemed like a nice, safe, compromise.

Tamsin was born later that year, 15th October 1999, a perfect healthy little girl who was filled with life and laughter, and offered an emotionally if not monetarily rewarding second career for me.

She was a happy baby, and I was filled with joy to be around her every day. When I needed a break I used my mother as a babysitter, and I was glad that she got to spend so much time with the granddaughter that gave her so much joy. Shortly before Tamsin's first birthday my mother was diagnosed with pancreatic cancer, inoperable, and died within eight months despite treatment.

I was devastated, but at least I had my daughter to soak up some of my grief.

Gary, meanwhile, had also started to find fault with his choice of career. Turns out he'd qualified as a lawyer with dreams in his head of long hours working as a pro-bono lawyer helping little old grannies, and short hours earning actual money dealing with fat-cat clients.

Instead, he worked in a corporate tax law firm, and the only little old grannies he ever saw were trying their hardest to avoid paying any tax on their massive earnings because God-forbid their non-hard-earned money should go to the betterment of society.

When there came the offer of a posting overseas, doing work that far more closely aligned with his original vision, Gary and I decided quickly to pack up and go to Thailand.

The lifestyle was so much cheaper there that even on one income we were comparatively affluent. I devoted my time to my daughter until she reached school age. When Tamsin was old enough to start attended the Chiang Mai International School and settled in with children from all over the globe, I started to cast around for something else to do.

That was when I first began to work in a volunteer capacity. There were aid organisations and community organisations that welcomed anyone who could read, write and fill out forms. I could do all of those things. It was fun to be useful again, and reassuring to know that if I woke up one Monday morning and really couldn't face going in to work I didn't have to. Not that the day ever came.

I started to extend my wings a little further, and became involved in the initialisation and extension of a nutrition programme throughout the area. When that required less input I started to work more closely with vaccine registers, and administration of both types. My co-workers seemed to think that I was a fully qualified nurse and couldn't believe that I would work for free.

Sunshine and lollipops. That was what Thailand was like to me. I know some in New Zealand think of it with happiness as a holiday destination, and others view it with horror as a drug sentence death-squad country out to trap hapless Australians and New Zealanders who didn't realise it was a bad thing to traffic drugs internationally. The poor things.

To me it was endless days working with people and making a difference in their lives. Seeing Tamsin coming home happy every day, getting a tan that made her blend in more with the local children. Seeing her sprout another foot of height in the short time we were there. Growing taller on happiness and love and exposure to things that she accepted as common practice which Gary and I would always class as foreign.

Gary blossomed with the responsibility that was part of his leadership. He grew into a true man instead of a confusion of enforced sympathy and misguided direction that he'd been back home. He started to take charge of everything instead of trying to reach a consensus. And I let him because it was fun to watch him, and he was never threatening. He was never "a man" in a way I needed to be scared of.

Our perfect, happy family growing strong in the midst of poverty and sunshine. We weren't living hand to mouth on fishing spots that had been handed down through generations. We weren't trying to sell bottled water to tourists on the beach. We were happy with our western jobs and our western expectations in our eastern home that was eight times bigger than anything we would've been able to afford back in New Zealand.

We weren't doing anything special that Boxing Day. We'd gone to Phuket for the holiday, and we'd had a big lunch for Christmas day and it was still sitting heavy in my stomach in the morning. Not true for Gary and Tamsin who'd insisted on eating thick sandwiches of bread filled with leftover ham and turkey.

I nibbled on a wing, and then threw the bone away with most of the meat still attached. It was time to start my annual diet anyway.

Gary went off into town to have a mosey among the stalls that were set-up for the tourists. He spent half his time in Chiang Mai insisting he wanted to be treated as a local, and the remainder nosing among everything with his tongue hanging out like he'd just popped over for the week on a visit. I shouldn't be surprised that he would act the same when we were genuinely on holiday.

I grew bored with sitting by the pool and decided to

take Tamsin on a walk up the road. It wasn't too hot this early, and I could use the exercise to remind my body that it should be eating breakfast right about now.

Tamsin skipped ahead on the road singing to herself. She followed a stray dog into the underbrush, and I had to run over to her before she adopted him as a pet. I don't have anything against dogs mind you, just the range of diseases being carried by this one seemed high on the register.

She cried a bit when I pulled her away, and I picked her up to carry her when she grumpily refused to walk. She was stubborn like her mother, and I knew from my experience upon others it was no use fighting her in this state.

Other people say they felt the rumble in the earth just minutes before. Because I was on the move I didn't feel a thing.

The first I knew something was wrong was when I heard a shout behind me. There was something off about it – it wasn't just the call of someone going about their usual day. I turned to look.

It took a while to make any sense of what I was seeing. There was water on the road. A mains burst? A sprinkler?

Before I could consciously put it together in my head I was running. Not along the road, that was level until the bend over 600m away. Straight into the underbrush at the side where my mind had registered there was an incline.

I turned for one last look just before the water hit. It was churning at the front. Pulling things under as it advanced. My mind flicked to the image of Gary and Tamsin coming down the fun slide at the water park a year before. He'd cradled her between his legs to make sure she didn't get hurt, and when they hit the pool at the end his weight propelled him over her and dragged her under. She'd emerged unharmed. Coughing with the water she'd expected to be air. She grumped along for a while before being caught up in the fun again. His weight had sucked her under. He'd had to pull her out of the water so she could breathe.

Just before the water hit I pushed Tamsin as hard as I could. I didn't have time to aim, but there was a clear spot to my side where she landed. The last expression I saw on her face was a look of horror. I can try to pretend that she was horrified at the water, just as I can try to proclaim I was acting in her best interests. But my mind falls back to the truth and the half-truth. She was horrified because I pushed her away to face the water alone, and in some part of my psyche I can't pull apart whether I was acting in her interests or in a last-ditch effort to survive.

Whatever.

It's not like I can go back and explain.

The edge of the water pushed me under and rolled me painfully along the road. The shock had taken my breath away. My lungs immediately screamed for air.

My head and body struck hard against a solid object. The push and pull of the water lessened and I thrust my head out into the air, the beautiful clean fresh wonderful air, and sucked in a breath.

I'd hit against a car, that had hit against a tree. They both gave way and I was once again pulled under the surface. Dragged under and crushed together with everything else the foul water had picked up. But not before I saw a small girl caught in the overhead wires that were now water level wires. One of the poles bottoms caught traction with the road surface and the wires pulled tight out of the tumultuous wave for a second. The body caught in a garrotte by the wires, pulled tight at the tiny child's neck. The tiny girl's neck. And then the wave pulled me under and the pole lost its grip, and we all tumbled back into the water.

It doesn't matter what you try to tell yourself.

Your mind's eye sees what it wants to see.

I pushed my daughter away in terror and she strangled to death a moment later.

I can't tell anyone the worst of the things that happen to you. I can't risk my loved ones hating me as much as I hate myself.

Murderer.

CHAPTER SEVENTEEN

'I'm outside. Can you not hear me knocking?'

I'd woken with an addled brain to the sound of my phone ringing. The night before I'd stayed late with Gary. I was convinced that I'd seen a sign of independent motion, and I wanted to stay and check for more. I'd only given in when I started awake and realised that I was only capable of viewing the inside of my eyelids.

Rena stood at the door. She looked like a breath of fresh air, compared to the smog of my dazed and tired eyes. A little girl clung to her leg.

I bent down so that I was level with the girl's line of sight.

'Hello. You must be Chloe.'

The tiniest corner of an eye peeked out from behind the safety of Rena's leg, but then whipped back when I smiled and waved.

Rena shrugged and smiled. 'It's not that she doesn't like you...'

'Come in. Have a seat. I'm about to make myself a coffee, fancy one?'

'Yes please.' Rena sat on the couch and patted the seat next to her. Chloe struggled with the deep leather cushions, but managed to crawl into position next to her mother. She promptly moved Rena's arms around her shoulders, and held her mother's hand in front of her face for protection.

'How's she doing?' I mouthed as quietly as I could.

Rena shrugged. 'Good,' she mouthed back then angled her face to look down at Chloe. 'It's so good to have you back safe and sound with us, isn't it my love?'

I saw the tiny movement of a nod.

'I tell you what honey. How about I leave you sitting here and give you this,' she pulled a large colourful book out of her handbag – a very hungry caterpillar emblazoned on the front, 'and I go into the kitchen and have a chat with my friend. Will you be okay?'

There was a series of soft whispers that I couldn't make out, but I believe the gist of the response was "Not on your Nelly." Nevertheless, after some more whispered negotiations, and pointing out the lack of distance to the kitchen, and the ease with which Chloe could see us both, Rena stood and made her way through to join me.

'She's okay during the day. Apart from the clinging,' she said quietly. The noise from the kettle sufficiently disguised her words from Chloe's ears. 'But she's having a really rough time at night. It takes me an hour or more to settle her in her room alone, and then I'll wake up during the night and she'll have crawled into bed beside me.'

I grabbed a couple of cups from the overhead cabinet and poured the newly boiled water into the filter for my machine.

'She must be having nightmares,' Rena continued. 'I can't see what else would wake her up at night, but she doesn't make any sound. She used to shout out and cry when she was having a bad dream, but now I can only tell because she gets into bed with me.'

'What does her therapist say?' Chloe was receiving free counselling through ACC. A specialist child therapist had been appointed to her, and she was on a regimen of four hours counselling each week.

'She's confident that she's making progress. It's just hard to trust her though.'

I put a hand on her arm. 'It's early days yet. I'm sure if you give it time you'll see improvements. And it may be that Chloe acts worse before she starts to get better.

Sometimes the therapy will make her confront things that she'll find difficult. It'll upset her, but it's also part of her recovery.'

Rena nodded, but her expression stated, "I've heard this all before".

'Is she coming along when you visit Ash?' He'd finally been sentenced for his part in the abduction. I think he'd welcomed the punishment just so he could work off his guilt. His prison sentence wasn't that long though. In another six months he could apply for home detention. His application for unsupervised visitation would take years longer, however. Maybe until Chloe was eighteen.

Rena nodded. 'I thought it would be difficult for her to adjust to the setting, but I don't think she cares. As long as she gets to see her dad she's happy.'

I poured out the coffee and added standard milk to mine. Rena screwed up her nose at the sight, and added a dash of cold water as she discovered I didn't have any trim in the fridge.

'I wondered what you thought about letting Sarah meet with her?'

'With Chloe's therapist?'

'No. With Chloe. I thought it might help her to talk with someone who'd been through the same thing.'

As I stared in horror at Rena I wondered how some people's brains were wired. How on Earth could she think that would be a good idea?

'I think you should run that one by Chloe's therapist before you do anything,' I said as calmly as I could. I kept my mental fingers crossed that her therapist would say no to that idea. Forever.

'Kendra suggested it,' Rena continued. 'She thought it might be good for the both of them.'

'I don't think it will be Rena,' I replied, trying to keep my voice level. 'If we were talking about somebody at the same age, or even someone who was older but had been in the same situation it might be worth a go, but Sarah was held for decades. I just don't think it's the same thing at all.'

'It didn't sound that great of an idea to me either,' Rena admitted. 'But I don't really know about all this therapy stuff. I didn't want to let it go if you thought it might really help.'

'I think what will really help is just you being there for her,' I said, my voice firm. 'Chloe will need your support for a long, long time to come. As long as you're willing to give it to her I don't think she'll need anything else.'

Rena smiled in relief. 'I can certainly do that.'

We moved back into the lounge. Chloe was tapping the hard-back book cover in a quick pattern before she turned each page. I noted that Rena reflexively responded with her own tap. I touched her arm to draw attention to it.

'That's something I would be able to help you with,' I said. 'If you want me to.'

There was a flash of fear on her face, but Rena glanced down at Chloe before turning back to me. To give up the tricks and games that OCD demanded was a long and challenging road. It required a strong focus. And strong trust that your shrink wouldn't lead you into danger.

'Okay,' Rena said putting her hand on Chloe's silky soft blond hair. 'Okay, I'd like that.'

***

I met up with Denise a few weeks after she'd been released from prison. On first meeting her I wished I'd got in touch sooner. She had changed since leaving prison. The angles on her face were harder. The lines on her forehead were almost gone, the skin stretched so tightly over the bones of her face.

'How're you doing?' I asked and leaned in tentatively to give her a hug. She responded by grasping me and squeezing me tight to her.

'I don't understand what's going on half the time,' she said bluntly. 'Everything looks different from when I was last here. Everything seems to move so quickly. I can't catch up.'

'It'll take some time, but you don't have to catch up all at once. How are you doing financially?'

'Okay. I've got a job in a dance studio. At the moment it's just assisting but the teacher thinks that they might have an opening for me to run a class by the end of the year.'

'That sounds good. How do you get on with the pupils?'

'Oh, they love coming up to me when the teachers got her back turned to talk in secret to "the murderer",' she said laughing. 'I get quite a kick out of it. One girl introduced me like that to her mother, and the look of horror on her face.'

'She really thought you were a killer?'

'No! She couldn't believe that the darling delicate girl that she insisted learn ballet to be more of a lady would be so uncouth as to mention my problems in public.'

I laughed with her as she showed me through into her kitchen.

There was hardly any furnishings in the house. Apart from the basic appliances it would've come with there was nothing more than a single picture on the wall.

Denise saw me looking and came over behind me. 'I had that in the cell as well. Not framed of course. My mother gave it to me for my sixteenth birthday. Before everything started to go wrong.'

The picture was a Dega print of a ballet dancer. The strong lines sparely tracing out the silhouette.

'It's beautiful.'

'I have tea or coffee,' she offered. 'Nothing flash. Just Bell or Nescafe.'

'A cup of tea would be great,' I replied and sat down in the kitchen to watch her move around. She hugged the middle of the room. I'd noticed it in prisoners before. They grew accustomed to such a small space that they had trouble utilising a larger area. It would go, of course. It was the adaptability of the human psyche that grew the habit in the first place, it would dispense of it the same way.

'Did you find out about the house?' Denise asked as she poured the tea out into the cups.

'It's empty. We can go there today if you want to.'

Denise stood at the bench and stared out into the side

yard. There was nothing there but a worn concrete path, a mildewed wooden fence, and the eave of the neighbour's house, but she stared intently.

'That sounds good,' she said as she reanimated herself and brought the tea tray to the table.

'It's a date.'

***

There had been drizzle in the morning, but it cleared as we reached Rangiora. The wipers screeched in protest until I turned them down a gear and then off.

I followed Denise's directions until she grew unsure, and then I pulled to the side of the road and turned on the GPS on my phone. I always found it confusing to look at an arrow travelling down the page when I was travelling straight down a road as I always was, but I passed it across to Denise to let me know when a turn was approaching.

She started to recognise the area again, and soon let the screen on the phone turn dark.

When she pointed out the house I carefully pulled the car into the driveway and edged it up to the side of the house. I cut the engine, and sat back in my seat, looking at the house. It was similar to the one that Denise currently rented, and I wondered if that was because she liked the style or if it was just due to her rent-scale.

'Are you ready,' I asked without turning to her. If she needed more time she wouldn't need me looking at her.

'I'll just sit here a minute or two I think,' she answered. 'Could you go on inside?'

I nodded, and got out of the car. I took an envelope out of my bag with the house-keys inside. A realtor's logo decorated the keytab in bright blue and white.

There were three keys on the tab. One was clearly for the garage, and by a process of elimination I found the correct one for the front door.

It was empty. Sitting and waiting quietly for the next occupant. Dust motes spun in a shaft of sunlight that cut through the rainclouds to brighten the day. It would soon clear and maybe even be beautiful and sunny. But for now one ray of sunshine would have to do.

I walked slowly through the property. It must only have been recently vacated. Any property in Christchurch or surrounds was snapped up as soon as it became available. Also there was the smell of occupancy in the air. The steam and odour from the last meal cooked in the kitchen. The humidity from the last shower in the bathroom.

I walked over to the dining room that looked out over the backyard. There wasn't much room. A couple of metres to the fence line and half of that filled in with a ring of bushes; camellias, another bush, another bush. There was also an old apple tree that had seen better days. Someone had attached a rope swing at one point, but the traditional half-tyre that would've formed the seat was missing rendering it useless.

I unlocked the back door, but didn't venture out there yet. This was Denise's show. I was just here as a spectator and a support.

It took another ten minutes before I heard the car door slam closed. There was a long moment of silence and then I heard her come into the house. She paused in the front rooms, and then came through to find me at the back.

'Are you ready to go through?'

Denise nodded and led the way. She walked over to a camellia that was almost fully white with occasional splashes of crimson.

'Here.'

I walked over to her side and stood with her, staring at the spot. There may have been signs of an old disturbance of earth, but it could just have easily been the years of raking up of dead flowers and foliage in between.

'I don't know what to do.'

I stared up at the sky. There were more clear patches showing now. The sun was starting to make progress on its mission to bathe the earth with warmth.

'What was his name?' I asked quietly.

'I didn't give him one.'

'How do you think of him? When you think of him.'

'My baby boy.'

'Then let's start there.'

Denise looked at me, her eyes glazing with tears, but her determination holding them in. She wasn't going to break that easily. Not this woman of determination and steel.

'My baby boy.'

There was a long silence, and I thought that maybe that was all the epitaph there would be. Perhaps that was all that there was to say. But I was too quick to judge. Denise sighed deeply and closed her eyes, and then resumed her speech.

'I miss you every day. I think of you every day. I'm sorry that I didn't think of you as much when I was pregnant with you. I should've been more careful.'

She knelt down and put her hand flat on the ground, then stroked it back and forth.

'I always thought you'd grow up to be something spectacular. The next Baryshnikov, maybe.'

She signed again and stood up. 'I never gave you that chance and I'm sorry. I'm sorry that you came too early. I'm sorry that I didn't look after your body when it was growing inside me instead of just looking after my body as I'd always done. I didn't give you a fair shot and you deserved one.'

Denise shifted from foot to foot and looked up at the sky. Although she wasn't wearing high heels she stood on her toes, giving the same shape to her legs.

'You had a little sister,' she continued. I stilled in surprise. Denise and I had spoken a lot since she started the release process, but she'd never said a word about Shelley.

'She was a beautiful little girl. A tiny little girl. She had the longest eyelashes I'd ever seen on a baby. And a mop of dark, dark hair. She was beautiful. Her head had squished out to the side when I gave birth to her, but I could tell that when she was given a week or two it would come back into a great shape. Beautiful.'

Another long pause. The sun was now hitting the top of my head. Warming up my hair until it felt like I had an electric blanket up there. I stroked it with my hand and it felt hot. Hot.

'I gave her to a man who raped me at a party. I knew better but I told myself it didn't matter. She was rubbish. She was the daughter of a rapist and she didn't deserve any better than what he could provide for her. I was messed up, and I messed her up.'

'I thought after you were born, that I would help her out maybe. I thought that I would have the chance when I started to feel better, to feel whole, to get her out of the mess I put her in and make her back into a child as she should be. Something to treasure and take care of.'

'And then you died and I knew I was no good. So I left her there,' she laughed a short bitter laugh. 'Turns out I wouldn't have been able to find her anyway. The police certainly couldn't. Not when it mattered to me. Not when it mattered for me. Nothing more than what I deserved though.'

'I thought it was a punishment for all the bad things I'd done. Going to a party I knew better to attend. Letting my attention slip from my dream once too often. I grew fat and lazy and I didn't look after myself and I didn't push myself enough, and that was why everything bad happened to me.'

'And everything bad that happened to me happened to you to, and to Shelley. I wouldn't do that now. But I didn't know better. I didn't know better until I was locked away and had the chance to consider anything except my own selfish interests. You had a selfish, selfish mother, and I'm sorry and I would give anything to have you back. To have you and your sister back. I'm so sorry.'

She was crying now, full on. I didn't think she would ever get that far, but obviously I knew nothing about the human psyche. What psychiatrist ever did?

'I'm going to live a better life now,' Denise continued. 'And I'm going to think of you and your little sister every day, and make sure the world knows that you both existed and you were both special.'

She paused and pursed her lips. 'Amen.'

I took her arm while we stood at the graveside for a while longer. Denise then went around the back garden picking a few flowers that were in full bloom and arranging them neatly into a loose bouquet. She lay it down on the ground and stepped back.

'I'm done.'

***

Terry leaned over and taped up the box with the masking tape holder. It ran out just before the end, but I came to the rescue with a few strips of Sellotape hastily torn off the roll with my teeth, and the lid stayed firmly closed.

I looked around the room. It had been well and truly emptied clean. Only the fixtures and fittings that were firmly attached to the house remained in place. Everything else was either with its new owners courtesy of Trade Me, sitting waiting for sorting and sale in the St Vincent de Paul storeroom, or packed away into the multitude of boxes that lay out in front of us.

'The movers are here,' Jacob called as he came back into the house.

'Well show them in. God knows it took them long enough to get here we don't want them sidling away when we're not looking.'

He popped back outside, and I cast a long look over Terry's face.

'What?' she asked irritably. Fitting her house into cardboard boxes hadn't left her in the best frame of mind.

'Just thinking how good you're looking lately. How do you feel?'

'Can you lay off the shrink-speak for a moment? I need a hand getting these outside.'

I poked my tongue out at her, and then helped her lift the first box out to the curb where three men stood idly by their truck looking as though it was their first day at work and no one had told them what to do.

'Are you all just going to stand there?' Terry called across to them, and when the men didn't move Jacob jumped to help us out instead.

'There are more boxes in the house,' Terry said as one of the men finally moved to relieve Jacob of a box and deposit it into the back of the van.

'In there,' she pointed when no one took an interest.

I thought for a moment that she would have to physically drag them into the house, but finally one sauntered off in the general direction of the house and his mates seemed to look after him with the idea that they may soon follow.

'God's sake. If I'd known I was going to end up doing all the work I'd just have hired a trailer from the Servo.'

It took me a moment to work that one out. Terry's Australian heritage lent itself to ending a great deal of words with 'O' which would more properly end with 'anything else in the dictionary'.

'Be a bit hard to get it back to the service station considering your end point.'

'Whatever. Careful!'

She ran off to reprimand one of the movers, and I watched her move. Despite the level of grump on her today, she looked years younger than she had when she was stalking Martin around the community. She moved easier, her expression was brighter, and the rapprochement with her son Jacob seemed to have clicked her back into her rightful place.

I would miss them terribly. On the other hand, what a great excuse for a trip to Australia.

'How do?' Kendra called out from the curb. 'Are they finishing up already?'

Terry appeared back in the driveway in time to hear and gave a loud snort. 'You'd be lucky. I think they've forgotten the way to their own van.'

I gestured to turn down the volume with one hand while failing to stop laughing. 'You might want to think about what you say. They are soon going to be in control of all your worldly possessions.'

'Is that your daughter?' Terry asked, ignoring my advice as usual and nodding at Kendra's car.

'That's her,' Kendra smiled as she too looked back. 'It's wonderful having her back again.'

Terry pursed her lips.

Kendra caught the look and nodded. 'Out with it?'

'Is she anything like the little girl you lost? It's been

so long.'

Kendra looked up at the eaves of the garage for a half-minute, then shrugged. 'It's been so long I don't know half the time how much she genuinely reminds me of my little girl, and how much is wishful thinking. But yeah. I think there are glimpses.' She sighed deeply. 'I just wish I'd found her sooner. Not just for all the time I missed, but for...' she waved her hand feebly.

'For all that she went through?' Terry suggested.

Kendra nodded. Terry reached over and pulled her into a surprise bear-hug. 'At least you get a chance to override that,' she stated firmly. 'You can put some good memories overtop of all that he did to her.'

I put my hand on Kendra's arm gently. 'Are you okay?'

Terry snorted again, and turned to go back into the house and do some more supervision. 'She never lets up. She was asking me exactly the same a minute ago. Just go back into psychiatry would you. Get paid for all your prying.'

I ignored her and continued to look at Kendra, but she just shrugged and smiled. 'I'll get by. She's having a bit of trouble sleeping, but during the day it's fine.'

'Do you want to go out after this? I haven't seen you much lately.'

Kendra looked surprised, and then shook her head. 'I want to take Sarah up to the Port Hills around Victoria Park. I used to take her there when she was little. Have picnics and sit in the sun.'

I nodded and smiled, but inside I felt a snip of jealousy. Kendra always used to be available for quick coffee, or a bite out. I missed it. I missed her.

'Aren't you going to invite Sarah over to help,' I asked and turned back to the moving truck.

'Go on,' Terry said, reappearing with another carton. 'Christine's dying to ask her if she's okay.'

I gave her the fingers behind my back as I walked back to the house to pick up a box and join in the fun. Kendra fell into step beside me. As she leaned forward to get a grip on the handles of a wooden chest filled with Jacob's old toys, her blouse rode up. There was a dark bruise, blue-black, in a large swathe over her side. She'd hit something, or been hit, hard.

'Come on out, leave it to the guys. Jacob's on his way out to give the keys to the realtor.'

I followed Terry back to the driveway and hugged Jacob hard. It would be a long time until I saw him or his mother again, and my eyes teared up.

'Give over,' Terry whispered, as I stepped back. 'Otherwise you'll have us all going.'

Ten minutes later Kendra made her goodbyes, and Terry and I stood in the driveway to watch her get into her car. Sarah was a dark slim shape in the passenger seat.

'She seems so different now her daughter's finally come home,' Terry said. Her voice sounded wistful, and I thought of my little Tamsin. Coming back from the dead. And how much I'd welcome her.

'Wouldn't we all be?' I asked as I watched them drive away.

***

'Terry's all packed up and ready to go. My little group is almost completely gone.'

Gary moved an inch in his bed. I looked with hope into his face, but there was still no recognition there. Of me, of himself, of his surroundings.

'I tried to see Ilene again as well. I got all the way through to the jail, went through all of the inspections, and then I just couldn't do it. All I could think of was her torturing her little girl. Breaking her skin. Breaking her bones. I can't forgive her for that.'

I paused for a moment as I tried to adjust myself. I didn't want to talk to Gary and tell him nothing but awful things. Where were all the bright happy occasions I should be telling him so he actually wanted to rejoin the human race?

Ilene's trial would be difficult. It would probably take more than a year to get set up, and even then it would be hard to prove. She was only on remand now because there was so much antipathy in the community, she'd be in danger if she was released on bail.

I don't know how the prosecution would be able to show that the injuries inflicted by Ilene were what had caused Angie's death, rather than those inflicted by Donald King. The police were only certain because of Sarah's testimony. Her recollection was that the child had died within a day of being brought by King to the house. Yet the injuries that led to her death were inflicted days earlier, and wouldn't have led to her death if they'd been treated.

It was possible that Angie had been taken earlier. King may only have brought her to the house when he realised that she was gravely ill. The last injuries may've been caused by him.

But the others weren't.

Injuries inflicted over years, and only a handful recorded in treatment. A break that hadn't been set by a doctor.

In the end it wasn't that Ilene was definitely guilty of Angie's death that stopped me from seeing her. But just the notion that she'd abused her daughter over years. And yet she'd attended our group every week with her devastation held out for inspection.

It was the betrayal that hurt.

'I might pop in and see Kendra again today. Since she's the only one left of the old group. I'm half tempted to get it all going again. I could pop in Denise where Ilene used to sit, and Rena in place of Terry.'

I stopped and laughed out loud.

'Or, you know. I could just meet my friends for coffee, or arrange for a girl's night out. Or in. Maybe it's time I left the group therapy out of my friendships.'

There was movement from the bed again as Gary shifted his legs. I'd actually come in with something to say to him. I didn't want to say it out loud, but that probably just meant that it was overdue.

'Gary. I meant to tell you...'

I trailed off. My chest was already beginning to tighten with anxiety. With fear. I looked at him lying there. His eyes still weren't focusing on anything. It will be the same as telling a stuffed toy your story. And there's the same likelihood of recrimination. Just do it.

'I never talked to you about the day that Tamsin died. I'm sorry. I should have shared it with you a long time ago. It's just... It's been hard for me to accept what happened that day, and I didn't want you to think badly of me. Of what I did.'

I stopped and took a deep breath. Here goes nothing.

I told him. At long last, I told him the truth.

EPILOGUE

The bodies of Kendra Little and Sarah Jones have been found dead inside Ms Little's Grahams Road property today.

Ms Jones, 41, was discovered on the lawn at the front of the property at just after 6:30 am this morning. Ms Little's body was later discovered inside, once police had gained access to the property.

Detective Senior Sergeant Erik Smith said police did not believe that the deaths were suspicious and that the matter had been referred to the coroner.

Police had notified the family and scene examinations were to continue throughout the week, Smith said.

"This matter is a tragedy, and a continuance of the violence that Donald King exacted towards this family. His kidnap and holding of Ms Jones for years against her will, and evasion of justice despite numerous inquiries by the Police and Ms Little, is a crime that will haunt our community for years to come. Ms Jones' survival through this terrible crime is a testament to her courage and bravery. My grief and condolences are with her surviving family and friends at this difficult time."

Ms Jones was held captive by Mr Donald King – the Christchurch Cradle Snatcher - for over 30 years after her abduction. She was one of only two surviving victims, the last remaining victim being Chloe Sutherland, aged four, who was rescued earlier in January of this year.

ABOUT THE AUTHOR

Katherine Hayton is a shy reticent genius who doesn't like to be put in the spotlight.

She has lived in Christchurch her entire life, and currently resides two blocks away from the house in which she was born.

Found, near water is her first novel.

CPSIA information can be obtained at www.ICGtesting.com
Printed in the USA
LVOW06s2133120315

430381LV00001B/19/P